AF303577

CALL THE MOTHERSHIP

OF DARK MATTER AND ASCENSION

Bibliografische Information der Deutschen Nationalbibliothek:
Die Deutsche Nationalbibliothek verzeichnet diese Publikation in der Deutschen
Nationalbibliografie, detaillierte Daten sind im Internet über dnb.dnb.de abrufbar.

Written by **Thomas Fèanis**
Concept by **Jörg Varga**
Cover artwork by **Lisa Artner**
Edited by **Peter Gordebeke**

Published by BoD - Books on Demand, Norderstedt

ISBN: 978-3-7407-5349-8

FOREWORD

BY THOMAS FÈANIS

Anyone would say that their story is a very personal one, and in doing so I'm aware of being cliche.

The concept for this book in not mine, it is Jörg's concept. This novel is the result of two people who decided to turn a concept into something that can be shared with everyone. Along the way it became something very personal for both of us.

Writing this story was challenging, not only because I have never written a novel before, but also because the topic itself is dear to me. It reflects a part of my own life, that now is embedded in the wonderful concept Jörg gave me. I wanted to do it justice.

Reliving my own past for this book, but more importantly the process of writing this book, is something that I am very thankful for and I feel honored to have been given the chance to do this.

My own hardships, as well as the hardships of this book's character, are a reflection of things each of us experience during the course of our lives in one way or another.

I wish you a lot of joy reading this book, and maybe it turns into your own story, just as it did for me.

ONE

HYPERSLEEP NIGHTMARES

Darkness - Silence.
Silence? No, not silence.

Slowly, a dull sound of destruction rises from the darkness and as the sounds around him grow louder and louder, his eyes opened to the sight of absolute chaos.

His cryocell stood open, but no one seemed to have opened it. He wasn't supposed to be awake yet, or was he? His head hurt with unnatural intensity, making it hard to think clear. He felt pain lashing throughout the left side of his torso, blackening his vision again for a brief moment. As he carefully touched the source of the pain, he noticed he was wounded. His fingertips where red – blood red.

Panic started to build up inside of him. Where was he? A thought struck him like lightening, being more horrifying than the wound and the lacking knowledge of his surroundings. Not only did he not know where he was, he did not know who he was. He was easy prey for the fear that had been sneaking up inside him, waiting for its moment. He panicked, his heartbeat increasing, thoughts racing through his head.

Who am I? Where am I? I need to get out. Concentrate – focus. You can do this. You can fucking do this! Get up, get out of this cell. MOVE!

In spite of his body aching from the numerous cuts and bruises he managed to leave his cell, only to be greeted by another horror.

Shit. Holy... shit.

The sight of bodies floating through the cryocell hold nearly made him fail to see that his own feet weren't touching the floor either.

Are they dead? No, not dead, just sleeping. For now.

At least that was what he allowed himself to think. Regardless of the state these floating bodies were in, he was the only one awake. The only one here. The only one. One. His name was One.

A rumbling, crashing sound rolled over him, like thunder shaking everything in the room. The cryocell hold was dimly lit by a handful of emergency lights, hindering him from seeing much beyond the bodies floating nearby. After his eyes adjusted, he saw cryocells with opened doors and others hanging loose in their mountings.

The thunderous sound returned and made One cover his ears. The cryocell hold shook more violently this time. Everything was spinning and for a moment One feared to lose consciousness, until he discovered an exit at the other side of the hold. A sign above the door read 'Crew Quarters'. Right next to it, another pointing in a different direction read 'Observatory'.

Crew Quarters? Observatory?

None of it made sense. From the corner of his eye he caught a glimpse of the flickering letters of yet another sign, 'Bridge & Command Centre' – that's when it all came back to him. A ship. He was on board of a ship. Not just any ship – the ship. The Mothership.

Another wave of noise hit the room, spinning and disorienting One, and leaving him helplessly drifting among the bodies of his fellow Crew members. His reality crumbled again as he desperately tried to hold on to something. Frantically, he tried to move towards the doors, or at least the floor, so the next wave wouldn't send him off floating among the bodies that may or may not be the corpses of the men and women who were considered The Crew. Reality faded as his mind tried to understand the situation he found himself in – his body drifting, arms and legs moving but not really getting him anywhere.

This is the end. That is how I die. Waking up just to be stuck in a room full of corpses. A weightless grave. My weightless grave.

He closed his eyes and gave in to the desperation that was waiting for him. This was the end. A brief journey this has been. So full of hope, so full of ideas and dreams. It meant nothing in this cold and dark place where not even the light wanted to grace anyone with its presents. One took a deep breath.

At least the life support system seems to be working. Good – I won't die because I am running out of air.

He hadn't even considered the chance of reaching a side of the room anymore, so it took him by surprise when he suddenly hit something, sending waves of pain throughout his already broken body. He had reached the bottom of the room.

Chairs and tables fixed to the floor, customary in interstellar ships, gave him the chance to move across the room in zero gravity.

Maybe this isn't over. Maybe I can escape this hell.

He needed to escape this grave.

Slowly One moved through the cryocell hold, using chairs and tables to get through the weightless cold see of hopelessness. One word ringing in his head, pushing him to move forward.

Escape.

TWO

HOW TO FALL WITHOUT GRAVITY

Escape. Again and again it echoed in his head. Escape. He grabbed another chair and pulled himself towards the table standing next to it. Above him the bodies were still floating, like a grotesque flock of birds, silently watching him advance across the room. The cryocell hold was still lit by flickering red emergency light. One could hear the roar of yet another explosion in another part of the ship. There had been a lot of them. Too many of them. The ship would not last much longer. But he couldn't worry about that right now – he had bigger problems at hand.

Getting out of the cryocell hold was all that mattered right now. Whatever had happened to the ship and its Crew, it wouldn't matter much if he joined the flock of silent bodies above him. Another thunderous sound wave past and shook the walls. One quickly pulled himself towards the next chair and held onto it until the shaking stopped. He felt exhausted, and every wave drained his energy reserves. He couldn't keep this up much longer. He grabbed another chair, continuing his way towards the exit.

The flock above watched him quietly. It felt like an eternity. Although he had noticed the room's size when he got out of his cryocell, it felt twice as big now that he had to slowly make his way across it to escape the hold. Another wave, another moment of terror – the fear of being catapulted back into the air. He desperately clung himself to one of the white chairs that filled the bottom of the room. He had tried to use one of the grey round tables in the hope that they would give him a better grip, but without success. He had learned very quickly that his only chance was to pull himself from one set of chairs to another.

The flickering lights above at the end of the room came closer and closer. He felt hope rising up inside him.

I did it. I made it. Only a little more and I'm out of here!

One focused all the remaining energy in his body to make it to the next set of chairs which surrounded one of the big round tables, marked with the red symbol of the Mothership.

Nearly there.

And then there were no more chairs. He had reached the last table and gazed upon a big space of empty hold that might as well have been the Grand Canyon he remembered from his time back on earth.

There was nothing to hold onto, which meant that another thunderous wave would surely be the end of his brief little journey. Fear filled his mind again. What was he supposed to do? He could never cover that distance fast enough. It was more than ten meters towards the doors.

If it wasn't for the lack of gravity, I could easily make that. What a fucking joke.

His wound started to hurt again. The aching had stopped as long as he had been focusing on the task before him but now that he was floating again, just barely holding onto the chair underneath him, he felt the pain rushing back into his body.

Fuck. What do I do? I need to get out of here!

He had only one chance. He knew it, but it scared him to death. He would have to make one last big pull towards the exit and hope that no shockwave would hit the room while he floated. There was no other option – no other way to do this.

I have to try. It's either this or die here, doing nothing. No, I will not let it end like this – not like this.

He focused one last time, gathering everything he had left in him and made one final big pull. He flew through the weightlessness, unable to do anything but to hope that his luck hadn't run out today.

It had not.

After what seemed at least a year he reached the exit door. He opened it and pulled himself through. He had made it.

I have done it. Holy shit, I have done it. I am still alive. I escaped! Now I can...

Now he could what? He had been so focused on getting out of the hold that he had not even thought about what came next. He stared at the big corridor in front of him. Which door had he even reached? Was it the one to the living quarters or the one to the observatory?

One didn't get much time to dwell on those thoughts when the power suddenly went out and darkness greeted him. If panic hadn't been already at his heels, now it definitely would be. He tried to get a sense of his surroundings – tried to see what was up and what was down, what's left and what's right. He couldn't. He saw nothing. And he panicked.

The air seemed to leave his lungs quicker than he could breathe in and suddenly the big corridor was nothing more than a tiny cube of blackness that he had been locked in. He tried to scream but no sound came out of his mouth, except for a miserable gurgle. It doesn't matter anyway, it was not like there was anyone to hear it. Or was there? Maybe there had been other survivors, some members of the Crew that were awake too?

Don't be stupid. The fucking power went out. There is no one. You are going to die. You made it out of the hold just to die in an empty corridor.

He gave up. There was nothing left he could do. Apathy started to fill his body and mind. Giving up was all that's left, right? Maybe he should just wait for the end to come. It mattered little what effort he had made. In the end he would just end up in another room of the ship. A room once filled with people, filled with excitement, with hope. Now nothing more than a dark grave. He thought about his loved ones, his friends, and his family. He could not remember a single face. The cryosleep must have some side effects. Who knew?

What a sad way to go. I can't even remember the faces of my friends. It's like I have been alone on this ship forever.

As the lights came back and the corridor was filled with the red emergency light once more, One didn't even move at first. He had his eyes closed. Why even try?

...because this is not how you're going to die! You hear me! Get your ass moving!

His brain was not ready for the sudden rush of adrenaline that hit his body like a freight train, but he started to move nevertheless. He had to move. Maybe there was someone else? Maybe he could stay alive just a little longer.

Suddenly something in the wall next to him exploded. Pain flashed through his body, his sight faded and he was hurled through the air against the wall on the opposite side of the corridor. As he slowly regained control over his body, he tried to move. A conductor had exploded, probably due an overload of energy, or the damage the ship had taken. He needed to move before another one of those explosions knocked him out for good.

Another explosion – this time a few meters ahead of him. It blew a hole in the corridor wall and hot steam was flowing out of it. What was causing those pipes to explode? Why now? There hadn't been anything like it back in the cryocell hold.

He tried to get closer to the wall so he could see what kind of pipe had exploded. It was impossible to figure out through the steam still flowing out of the hole. He couldn't really see anything besides some sparks, which indicated that the electronics of the ship were slowly starting to overload or that the damage was spreading throughout the conduits across the ship.

It can't be long before the life support system will shut down. Then we are really fucked.

The ship would do anything to keep the life support system running as long as possible. Even if it means shutting down entire areas to preserve the more important ones.

Areas like the one I am in – shit.

As if the ship had heard his thoughts, the door at the end of the corridor began to close itself. One tried to move as fast as he could. The red lights flickered and there was another explosion behind him. The door was slowly closing and One was nowhere near it. The corridor was longer than he had estimated and there was no chance of him reaching that door. With a sharp hiss the door closed and the emergency seal came down, making it impossible to open it.

Although he had expected as much, the sight of door behind him being shut as well gave him another taste of bitter desperation.

Great! I can't move forward, I can't go back. I am fucking stuck.

There wasn't much time to dwell on that. He knew as much. With the doors shut down, he would need to get out of there somehow before he'd run out of air.

Frantically he turned around, trying to figure out a way to escape. That's when he noticed the small hatch on the right wall of the corridor. It must be one of the hatches to the repair tunnels lead throughout the whole ship. There was his chance to escape.

Ok, fine. Let's do this.

He quickly reached the hatch that was embedded in the grey corridor wall. It was shut tight, just like the doors. He was completely locked in. One didn't even bother to get angry. At this point his resolve was broken. He was desperate.

Of course you are sealed, you fucking asshole hatch!

He closed his eyes and took a deep breath, realizing how thin the air was becoming. It was pure luck that saved One from losing his eyesight when the wall in front of him exploded. With his eyes still closed, the shockwave of the explosion took him by surprise. He was hurled around like a leaf in autumn and when he hit the floor, forcing out the remaining air in his lungs. Ringing for air and trying to remain conscious, he tried to gain control over his body again. When he opened his eyes, he couldn't do anything else but laugh. A desperate, nearly insane laugh.

The hatch was open – because there was no hatch anymore. The wall had been torn apart by the explosion, leaving busted pipes, destroyed cables and electronics out in the open. Like a cosmic joke the entry to one of the repair tunnels was laying before him, like it was always meant this way.

One didn't hesitate. He crawled into the tunnel and pulled himself forward, not looking back. He went down another hatch, up another ladder and in doing so lost track of time. Cables were hanging down, hatches half open, as if they weren't able to close in time before losing power. Parts of the tunnels were completely destroyed so he had to find alternative routes. Red emergency light was the only light he had. In the distance explosions continued their rumbling. Slowly but steadily, he worked his way forward through the innards of the ship.

When he thought that he could not continue anymore after opening another hatch, he finally saw it: An end, an exit. Ahead of him there were no further hatches or ladders leading him to another repair tunnel, but an opening into a room. He gained speed as he hurried towards the opening. It felt like it had been years since he got out of his cryocell.

One last pull and he was suddenly flowing in an open space. If he had thought that the cryocell hold had been big, this was another dimension. He found himself in the rear observatory of the ship – he remembered this room. Unline the observatory in the front section of the ship, the rear observatory was large and functioned as the main observatory of the ship. It was grand indeed. The observatory didn't have the grey walls like the rest of the ship, its walls were completely made out of glass. The sight that it offered was one of a kind. The whole universe seemed to be laid out in front of him. He could see the stars clearer than he would have ever dreamed of. Galaxies waiting to be explored, stars collapsing in the far away depths of the universe and the secrets hidden behind the borders of the known space itself – it all was right before his eyes. A sight so beautiful there were no words to do it justice. How small he seemed, floating through the grand hall of the observatory, like an insignificant speck of dust in the face of the never ending mystery of the universe.

The big pillars supporting the grand hall made the towers back on earth look small, they looked like monuments from another time. Majestic and silent they stood vigil, holding their breath in front of the holy goddess of the universe. His eyes gazed into the endless depth above him. Time seemed to stop and One had no idea how long he had been drifting beneath the mighty pillars of the observatory. When he finally came back to his senses, he remembered why he was on board this ship, why he was on board the Mothership.

I wanted to see it. I wanted to see the mystery of the universe itself, I wanted to see what lies beyond the stars – uncover the secrets that are waiting for us. I wanted to be on this ship because it was the beginning of something bigger than myself or anyone I have ever known. I will not let it end here. I have to save this ship. I have to figure out what is happening

One made his way to the other side of the observatory. He passed the centre, a small cube with a big telescope to look for distant destinations. He knew there had to be gravity down there, but he could not stop now. He had to figure out what was happening.

Fear and determination battled each other as One made his way across the observatory. His goal was clear, although he had no idea how to reach it or how he would be able to manage everything on his own. But he had no choice. The stars were shining down on him, the pillars stood reverentially. He felt lost, alone and insignificant. But he had to move forward. There was no other choice.

THREE

OF DARK MATTER

A bulkhead awaited him when he finally made his way across the observatory. One didn't hesitate. There was no time to lose, and he had to keep moving. As soon as he reached the other side, artificial gravity set in. The sudden change made his stomach twist – his legs were shaking. The rush of adrenaline that had kept him moving started to fade and his body began to realize the extent of exhaustion he had endured.

One couldn't hold himself up anymore and his legs gave in to the temptation of rest. He sank to the ground and as much as he tried to fight it, he could not stop his body from breaking down. The adrenaline was gone, he was tired and the pain of his wounds returned even stronger now that he wasn't in zero G anymore.

Lying on the floor, breathing heavily, One tried to gather the strength to get up again. He couldn't.

I have to get up again. I have to... but I can't... I just can't. Maybe if I just sleep for a little while – just sleep...

His surroundings started to fade and the sounds of the ship became dull and drifted farther and farther away. He knew it was a bad idea to sleep right now but his body couldn't go on any further, not without any kind of medical attention, equipment or at least provisions.

His body was nearly lost to the darkness around him, the cold floor underneath him and the exhaustion of the last hour, when all of the sudden a single sound made his way to his fading mind. It was not one of ship's the sounds he had heard since he woke in his cryocell. It wasn't even a mechanical sound, but something far more thrilling.

Are those... voices?

His mind snapped out its journey to unconsciousness and he was suddenly wide awake.

Voices – those are human voices!

Although his body was nowhere near being ready to get up again, he forced himself to get back on his feet. There it was again – the sound. He tried to follow it, taking little steps towards it. He couldn't see anything in the darkness that engulfed him, but with every step it felt like the voices became louder and louder. As he made another step forward he could see a light in the distance, dim, but it was there.

One slowly made his way towards the light, taking steps with shaking legs that were still confused by the gravity. The light grew brighter as he continued. Could it be that there were others – other who were alive as well? Maybe he wasn't alone after all. One hastened up his movements and tried to get closer to the source of this dim light in the distance, excited by the possibility of meeting another human being in this nightmare.

As he was close enough to make out the source of the light, his mind was hit by a wave of desperation and frustration. No humans, no passengers, just a holoscreen mounted to the wall. He was close to breaking down again, but forced himself to move on. It was probably just a projection of some kind of emergency protocol, but he couldn't give up on his last hope that someone was reaching out to him from some other part of the ship.

Please don't let this be another disappointment. I need something to keep me going. Please, just... something.

As he reached the screen, he silently thanked whatever higher existence was out there in the universe. There were faces on the screen, people trying to communicate with him. He made his final steps towards the screen. He instantly recognized them – those were the faces of the Mothership Crew. They were all there: Sid the Primer, Ermis the Jetsetter, Schachinger the Soundshaper, Fèanis the keeper of the Codex, Commander Swayton and the Overmind himself, Jörg.

The faces on the screen eased up as they were able to see One. He could hear all of them breathe a sigh of relief at the sight of him, but something else flashed on their faces – worry.

I must be in terrible shape if they look at me all worked up like that.

Jörg slowly started to talk: "It is good to see that you are alive. Listen carefully – something inside the ship has caused this. We are not really sure what it is, but we are sure of the danger we're all in."

"At the beginning it was just a small singularity," Commander Swayton continued, "but it got stronger and stronger over time, sending waves of energy through the whole ship. We had to shut down the systems or the amount of energy from this thing, whatever it is, would have destroyed the ship and all of us with it. We were drifting through space and got trapped in the gravity well of some sort of energetic fog. We are slowly getting pulled to its core and if the ship reaches it, the radiation will melt the mantle of the ship and you know what that means for us."

The faces of the others got even grimmer.

"We cannot clearly localize the source of this thing," Fèanis said with a hint of anger in his voice, "we can only narrow it down to the part of the ship it comes from, and show you the way. You are the only one who can save this ship right now, all the others are either sleeping, locked in behind emergency doors or... worse."

Jörg looked at him with pure concern. He was clearly worried about One. "The bridge is sealed off. We cannot get out to help you with this mission. We can only give you directions and talk you through the ship's communication systems. We cannot hear you – it's one-directional only. I am deeply sorry. We will help you the best we possibly can and give you all the equipment and intel we have to get you through this   but you have to do this by yourself."

They can't possibly be serious! They can't really expect me to do this by myself? This is insane!

"First, you will need medical care," Jörg continued. Suddenly a number of lights went on, filling the room with bright white light. He could make out a few equipment storage units – one of them was a medical storage room. ""You can find everything you need in there. Take your time and then make your way to the shown location. You can do this. We all believe in you, we all depend on you. Again, I am sorry, but there is no other way to get out of this. You have to do this yourself."

The shock of everything that had been revealed to him made One numb. For a moment he couldn't move.

I can't do this. I just can't. I am not the person to get this job done. I will fail them – I will doom us all...

"You can do this," Fèanis said with a calm voice. "We all know you can," Ermis added. The rest nodded encouragingly. One looked at them, took a deep breath and started walking towards the storage rooms.

There is no other way. I have to do this.

After he tended to his wounds, he grabbed the multifunctional equipment he needed and got himself a number of light sources for the darker sections of the ship. One also put on a protective suit, and got himself a backpack with water and a handful of energy bars and protein snacks.

He followed the light on the ground that showed the way to the next destination, which turned out to be a chute that looked more like a hole without bottom to him. He knew what it was. This was the main plenum 1313, or as the Crew called it: The Dante Tray.

Part of his brain began to realize the magnitude of this task. It would be a journey into the dark, with dangers and a very real possibility of failure and death. His only companions were the flashlight in his hand and the hushed voices inside his helmet that gave him directions. As he slowly began his descent into the darkness below, One could only think of a sentence he had read back on earth in a life that seemed so far gone: Abandon all hope, ye who enter here.

FOUR

SHAPESHIFTER

Abandon all hope who ye who enter here. The words kept ringing in his head as he made his way deeper and deeper into the endlessness that was the Dante Tray. The only light sources in his sight were the guide lights that showed him the way. What other way was there except down? He had been climbing down for what felt like hours.

Hours? Or days? Feels like I've spend my whole life climbing down this fucking shaft.

One knew that the Mothership was not a small vessel, but a giant and massive object. He felt exhausted carrying on, although that feeling could as well be normality. What was there except this endless descent?

What made the whole trip down the Dante Tray even worse were the occasionally destroyed skywalks he had to bypass. That was made worse by his lack of light to really see everything in his path, and they often tended to just cut out. From time to time One found himself in complete darkness. At first he stopped and waited until the lights came back on or used one of the light sources from his backpack, but he soon realized that this in fact cost him more energy than just continuing with his descent. A small part of him started to hope for his feet to miss a step so the torture was finally over.

He came across another closed bulkhead.

No use in trying to force it open, I guess.

The last few attempts resulted in nothing. One realized after the third sealed bulkhead that his energy was too important and every second he struggled with an effort to open a sealed bulkhead, wait for lights to go on or frantically search his backpack for another light source was a bad use of his energy. He had to be smart, he had choose which of the possible actions deserved his energy.

He traversed another small tray that led him to a route around the closed bulkhead and exited on the other side of the shaft. It was the easiest way – it was the fastest way. One didn't know how much time he actually had to complete his mission, the Crew had not revealed anything but he had a strong feeling that it wasn't as much time as his broken body demanded from him.

Down in the dark, One could make out the pale light of another holoscreen.

At least this one works. Another broken one and I would be in trouble.

Not that he really needed the short briefings the Crew gave him, but it was good to see their faces and hear their voices. At this point he didn't care whose voice he heard, he just wanted to be assured that there were other human beings on board this ship beside himself. Every time he had come across a broken holoscreen – and there had been a lot – his spirits sank, because he felt lost and lone. He felt so alone. One would have given anything to speak to another human being, to touch another living person, to not be alone in this endless shaft, climbing down and going insane all by himself – but there was no one else but him, he was alone.

The briefing was short and redundant. Down. Further down the Dante Tray. Abandon all hope who ye who enter here.

Fatigue began to take over. With each step he took it became stronger. First it made his legs clumsy and slow, he had to watch for every step. Now his hands began to fail him. Even closing them became more and more difficult.

I need to take a break – just a few minutes. I can't go on like this.

He saw an alcove a few meters below him. It was not very big, but a person could fit in it.

It'll have to do, right? What other choice do I have?

The last steps towards the alcove seemed like a whole other dimension of hell. He was very close to collapsing and there was no chance he could go any further. When he finally got to his resting place, all he could do was sit down and close his eyes. His backpack beside him, the flashlight turned off.

Just a few minutes...

When he opened his eyes again he felt disappointed. A small part of him still hoped for this hell to be just a dream, but instead the darkness inside the Dante Tray greeted him.

He looked down the shaft with his flashlight turned on, because the guide lights weren't working properly in the upcoming section. There was another skywalk to cross, but something about it made him freeze for a second. It was a regular skywalk like the ones he had already crossed, but still there was something odd about it. When One realized what it was that irritated him and he nearly fell down the shaft because he leaned forward in excitement and a pure adrenaline rush.

Something on this skywalk was moving. It was a person. A human being who slowly made its way across the skywalk, handling every movement with great caution.

One lost no time. He got on his feet, took his backpack and began climbing down as fast as he possibly could, not paying attention to the danger of falling.

As he got closer to the Skywalk he stopped to wave at the stranger. He shouted too but quickly realized how stupid that was, since he still had his helmet on and the stranger was not close enough to hear him. He continued to move but paused every few steps to wave and make gestures towards the person on the skywalk.

It seemed that not all luck had abandoned him because at one point the stranger began moving faster and was definitely looking in his direction. One had reached the skywalk and looked towards his new found hope. The stranger was moving towards him, making their difficult way across the damaged traverse.

Finally the stranger reached One. Behind the visor of the helmet, One could make out a man in his early 30s. He had brown eyes and a big nose, and One could make out streak of light brown hair too. He didn't really care about anything besides the fact that this was another person standing in front of him. He no longer was alone.

"Hello!" One said a little too excited. "I am... I am One! Did you come from another part of the ship? I've been out here climbing and making my way down all alone. I spoke to the Crew, they sent me on a mission to save the ship. I was sure I would be the only one, but it's good to see another human being..."

One took a deep breath. From the look on the strangers face he had been talking very fast. The stranger looked at him for a couple of seconds then began to speak. "Hello One. It is good to meet you. I thought I was alone out here too. I awoke in a cryocell in the great hall in block D and everything was just chaos. There were dead people and explosions and I made my way out of there as quickly as I could. From what I see you come from Block A right?" He managed to pull a tired smile on his face. "Now about that mission. I have one as well. Why don't you tell me about yours and maybe we can help each other out."

One took a look at the stranger and his outfit. It was the outfit of Block D, that much was correct and he had a name tag with his voyager number on it. It spelled "Shape'. Something about the named seemed very familiar. He had seen that name before. It felt like the name triggered something hidden inside his brain, but One couldn't really get a hold of it. All he knew was that he had heard and seen that name before.

Even if I haven't met him before, it doesn't matter. Why am I even looking if his cloth and nametag are in order, who cares?! I should be happy to see anyone out here.

With that thought giving him confidence he began to tell the man about everything that had happened since he woke up in that cryocell.

He had been talking for a couple of minutes and finally came to the part of his story, where he had decided to rest and saw someone moving on the skywalk beneath him. Shape looked at him, silently listening to everything and nodding his head in agreement during parts of his story.

"Well, One, it seems we both have the same mission here. I as well talked to the Crew and they gave me the same orders. We have to find out what's causing all this. It's good that I found you. Together we can achieve much more and figure this out. If we trust each other we will get out of this alive. I promise you."

One felt waves of hope rushing through his chest. He wasn't alone anymore. There was someone to help him, a friend to walk beside him. "Yes," he said, "let's trust each other and get through this hell together. I am happy to have found you. I thought I was going insane all by myself." One laughed in relief. "Let us get going and fix whatever it is that is causing this mess. It shouldn't be much further to the end of this shaft."

"Actually we don't need to climb all the way down," Shape said, "there is another way to reach the end. We won't have to waste that much energy and it's safer!"

One looked at Shape, but it didn't take him long to think about it. "Ok," he said, "if you think so. We need to trust one another, right? So... I guess, I follow you?"

"Yes, we need to trust one another. Just follow me," Shape grinned.

Instead of going down the shaft, Shape opened a small hatchway and started to crawl into it. One followed him.

Again, One had to crawl through the innards of the ship. They made their way through small pipes and bulkheads, taking one turn after another. Sometimes they went up just to go down a few minutes later. Shape never paused or looked around – he seemed to know exactly what to do and where to go.

Throughout the whole time he talked to One, ensuring him that it was not much further and that they were close to reaching their goal. Shapes voice comforted One and gave him strength to carry on. Although there were a few moments when One was confused because he had no idea where they were, Shape always found the right words to take away any doubts or fear.

"Just trust me – I know this ship very well. I studied the plans back on earth and the Crew ensured me that this way is much shorter."

"But why didn't they tell me?" One asked.

"If you don't know the ship this well, you would get lost immediately, so the Dante Tray was the obvious choice for you. It's longer but you cannot get lost," Shape smiled at him. It was a warming and trusting smile. "Don't worry, my friend. We will make it. It's not far anymore."

Friend – yes. Better to have a friend and not knowing where you are, then go down this hell hole again on your own. It's true, I don't know the ship well, the Crew probably knew this. They know everyone. I am so lucky I ran into Shape.

After while the space they had been crawling in for some time became bigger until both of them could stand upright. In front of them was small door, but its control panel was clearly out of power. It didn't respond at all when Shape touched it. There was a small window through which they could see the next room, but there was no way see anything else than darkness. Their flashlights just reflected in the window so they couldn't see what lay beyond.

"Damn," Shape sighed, "it seems we have a problem here, One. This control panel has no power."

"So can't we do anything? We can't go back now!" One started to panic.

"No, no. Calm down. It's ok. All we need to do is use the energy pack in your backpack and get the controls running again. As soon as the door opens I go through and reroute the energy to the panel on your side. It's a two-man job – easy. We've come this far, how hard can this be?" Shape grinned at One, making him smile too.

"Yeah," One said, "how hard can this be?"

"See?" Shape laughed. "Don't worry. We made a lot of ground and we are so close. This won't stop us. Together we can do anything, right?"

"Right!" said One.

They adjusted his energy pack and linked it to the power panel. A few seconds later it started to blink and beep. Shape opened the door and quickly went through it. As soon as he was through the door shut itself again. Shape simply needed to reroute the energy to his controls again in order for him to open the door.

The only problem was that One's side of the door never got any power. The control panel was black again. Suddenly, One heard a hissing noise from the other side of the door, followed by a clicking sound. The door locked itself from the other side. *What the...?!*

"Shape!" One yelled frantically. "The door has sealed itself? You need to reroute the power – Shape!" Panic started to overwhelm him. He stepped towards the window and what he saw made him gasp in shock.

On the other side of the window the lights had turned on. One looked into the inside of an escape pod. At the front of the vessel the pilot chair slowly turned around as the escape pod slowly undocked. Shape was sitting in his chair, looking at him. There was nothing human-like left in his appearance as the creature slowly stood up and walked towards the window. Its suit wasn't visible anymore. Its skin was as black as outer space. The form of this creature wasn't like anything One had ever seen, it was there but at the same time he couldn't make out the exact shape of it. Two dark holes rested in what appeared to be the head of the creature and One could barely see two dim red glowing points inside of them. Looking directly back at him. As it reached the small window, One could swear the creature was grinning. An empty, cold and frightening grin that was everything but human.

As the escape pod disappeared in the distance, One sank down on the floor and started to cry. He was alone again. Lost. Without energy and any clue where he was. No guide lights, no Crew to tell him where to go. The darkness welcomed him back like a lost child and as tears rolled down his cheeks One could hear a voice in his mind, the voice that had comforted him moments earlier and was now mocking his very existence.

FIVE

THANATOS

The tears had dried up. One sat on the floor, leaning against the heavy door. He could feel the big and cold emptiness of space reaching out to him. The shapeshifter was long gone. He was alone.

One starred into the big emptiness of the corridor. His gaze not focused. He stared into the big void that now filled his mind. He knew he had to get up again and make his way back to the Dante Tray. If only he hadn't lost so much time. How stupid he had been, how easily he had been tricked. A spark of hate silently rose inside him – a tiny little flame of hatred and rage.

He slowly rose to his feet – body aching as if it had been torn apart and stitched together again. His feet were sluggish and he had to force every step. How could he ever manage to find the way back? All those corridors, service pipes and small trays. He should have paid more attention to the turns they had taken on their way here.

I was too weak to see it, tricked by his words. This damn Shapeshifter.

Curse him and the place he came from. I shouldn't have trusted him. I should have...

It didn't matter anymore. The shapeshifter was gone and he had to carry on. He swallowed the rage and anger and continued.

Another closed bulkhead, and the door next to it didn't open either.

I have no idea how to get back. I don't even know where I am right now. For all I know I could have been going in circles the whole time. No – I definitely am moving forward... just where am I headed? There is no way I am finding my way back to the Dante Tray.

One sighed in frustration and punched the wall next to him. Pain shot through his fist, but he didn't care. He was hurting and he was lost, with no idea how to get back.

There has to be a way to get back. I remember some parts it. I just need to find one familiar service pipe or tray and I am on the right path again.

Service pipe E3458 – he knew this one! That was one of the pipes they had taken on their way here.

How did this creature know where to go? I am a member of the Mothership and I have no idea where all this exits and trays lead.

One didn't know how in the world the Shapeshifter found his way through the ship to the escape pod. There were signs leading to the escape pods, but they had not come across any. The shapeshifter knew exactly where to go to avoid them. He had planned this. His mind wandered, trying to figure out how the creature could have been on board of the ship. His head was spinning. He couldn't make sense of anything. There weren't enough answers to the questions that where bothering him so much.

Service pipe E3458. At least he was on track again – or so he thought. As he opened the door to the next room, nothing was familiar. Although he had seen the service pipe, he had no idea where to go next. The two doors in the small room were visibly broken and One knew he wouldn't be able to open them. All that was left was a bulkhead at the other end of the room, and he had no idea where it would lead.

I am lost anyway – as long as I am moving forward, I have to get somewhere eventually.

As he tried to open the bulkhead he screamed out in frustration. It didn't budge.

His voice echoed through the empty trays and corridors beneath and above him. He was surrounded by so many different paths but they all seemed to lead nowhere. His fist clenched and his jaw tightened – anger and rage rose again. The tiny little flame became a wildfire and took over his body.

He screamed, he shouted, punched the walls, and kicked the shut bulkhead. Nothing changed. Frustrated and in rage One screamed at the smartcams that were installed above the doors and bulkheads. He knew they probably didn't even work at the moment but it didn't matter.

"I should have stayed there!" he shouted, his voice trembling with despair. "I should have stayed on Gaia! What is all your fucking freedom worth now?!" No answer. His screams where swallowed by the emptiness of the ship. "I should never have come with you..." One sank to his knees and leaned his back against the cold thick metal wall. His head in his hands he felt overwhelmed by the lack of hope and perspective.

I could have stayed home. I knew they were lying to me, but at least I was happy as long as I stayed blind to their lies.

The Puritans had offered everything as they spun their web of illusions. Back on Gaia they had blinded the sight of their followers and given everything to maintain their fake bubble of happiness and security. One had been one of those blinded. He was insignificant, but happy. There was nothing he could be upset about, every burden and all worries had been taken from him. Eventually he figured out that it was a lie and the Crew had showed him the size of the false world he had been living in. He was so eager to join them back then. Their cause to find the truth had seemed more than just.

...and what has it brought me? All this freedom, searching for answers? Maybe I won't even see tomorrow.

From a very distant corner of his mind a very quiet but persistent voice started to hiss at him. "Maybe you are the mistake," it said. "Maybe you were the parasite in their midst all along, poisoning their hope and their mission. Look at you, you are nothing, lost and so alone. What is your worth?"

What am i worth?

One couldn't remember. He couldn't remember why he was here. He tried to focus, but it was like a section of his mind was blocked and shut off. Perhaps a side effect from his cryosleep?

Maybe he was the parasite indeed. Maybe he was the shadow being cast on this ship. Why else would he be all alone. Maybe he was the false element in the middle of the bright future that they had been hoping to find.

He looked down at his suit and the gear he had dropped on the floor next to him. A flashlight had fallen out of the backpack.

Something about it was so awfully familiar but he didn't know why or how. He picked it up and looked at it.

Who am I? Why am I here?

He tried to turn on the flashlight to get a closer look at the bulkhead, but nothing happened. He shook the flashlight and tried to turn it on again. Nothing. He threw it a corner of the room amrgily, only to instantly regret his outburst. He needed every bit of gear he had.

As he picked up the flashlight from the ground it suddenly shone bright as One held it towards his face, the beam of light hitting his eyes directly.

It took him by surprised and for a short moment he could only see the bright, white light that was burning itself into his head like the heat of a thousand suns. He was blinded and dropped the flashlight in shock, slamming his head against the wall behind him.

Falling to the floor in an inferno of bright light and pain something in his mind broke free. A realisation that broke free some pieces of his memory. He remembered why that flashlight looked so familiar. He had been using that same flashlight before. On a mission. A mission he had been a vital part of.

The mission... how could I forget this?!

The part of his memory that had been blocked revealed awful events in the past that made him gasp for air as the panic slowly overtook him in waves.

The mission...

"Good, you are awake. I hope the cryosleep hasn't left you with any too disturbing side effects?" Jörg looked at One with a smile. "We worried that something might go wrong with the whole procedure of waking you up from your little slumber early. You see, there can be some side-effects that are rather... unpleasant. One of the most common ones would be the memory loss, leaving basic body functions intact but blocking parts of the memory which can result in a temporary loss of identity. You are fully aware of yourself and your personality and history, right?"

One nodded shortly.

"Excellent," Jörg's smiled. "The memory loss wouldn't be permanent anyway. It mostly fades after a few hours – a day maximum. Oh, and we are so sorry for not offering you a good ol' cup of coffee." He winked at One while leading him to the small group waiting in the conference room. The rest of the Crew was sitting around the table eying him with curious eyes.

"Our Xenotechnician is up on his feet, I see. Looks fresh to me," Fèanis said with a grin on his face. "Wouldn't you agree, commander? Sure looks better than the rest of us."

"I wouldn't go as far as to say better, you know, but according to the hours we have been awake and working, I'd think we totally look like shit by now," the commander said while looking at Fèanis with an amused glance in his eyes. His words held some truth because the Crew did look exhausted. How many hours had they been awake? Had they even been in their cryocells at all?

"Speak for yourself! Ermis, Sid and me sure look fine as hell," Schachinger chuckled, as he gave Ermis and Sid a very meaningful look. They all were clearly trying to cover up the fact that they had some concerning matters on their minds.

"You have to excuse my Crew," Jörg said, still smiling. "They seem to be concerning themselves more with their looks rather than worrying about the matters at hand. Speaking of which..." he pointed at the two free seats at the round table.

As they sat down, a projection of a city map appeared on the table. Jörg looked at the map and then gave Commander Swayton the sign to start the briefing.

"This is the temple city Bashara on the planet Spurius Via II. We have received a very strange reading from a location in the city. The readings suggest a very strong energy source and although we are not sure on what the source actually is, we are very confident that it will be a valuable asset to our journey."

Jörg nodded in agreement. "That is why we need to explore the city and find the energy source. According to our scans, there should not be any kind of life in the city itself, which means we won't have to deal with possible aggressive encounters with the locals. We still need to be very careful though because we don't actually know what is awaiting us down there. Each step of the mission is to be taken with care. That goes for all of you."

Jörg looked around the table and rested his friendly but firm gaze on Fèanis a little longer than everyone else. Fèanis met his eyes with an amused smile, but One caught a glimpse of a tense and aggressive expression on his face.

The others nodded and each of them focused on the map that continued to show details of the city.

"Well, this should be a rather pleasant trip. The ship, as

awesome as it is, still bores the hell out of you when you're trapped here for too long," Sid said while slowly standing up from his seat. "I'll check if everything is ready for our little adventure. Ermis you fancy helping me?"

"Do I have to? I mean it's important and all, but it's still you and the smell is just unbearable!" Ermis ducked away as Sid playfully threw a punch at him. They both left the room going over different kinds of equipment they'd be using on this mission.

Schachinger got up from his seat and said, "I'll get down to the transport ship to see if everything is in order. I hope we can depart soon. This whole sitting around and waiting makes me a little tense."

Fèanis stood up as well. "Ok then I am off too. I'll check the armoury and the weapon systems. I know there isn't a living thing down there but I don't trust this city. Shit's not empty that long if there isn't something foul going on down there." He gave Jörg a very serious look and One couldn't help but think that the two of them probably had one or two arguments about whether or not they should actually go through with this mission or not.

"I will study the map some more. We need to be very sure about the path we take to find the energy source and how to come back safely," the commander said. Swayton studied the map with a deep look of concern on his face that made One shift uneasily in his chair. Jörg seemed to notice it. "Don't worry. We will be alright. After all, we have thought this through very carefully. Come – I'll take you to the dock."

One stood up and smiled, but he couldn't shake off the feeling that this was going to be much more serious than the Crew wanted to let him know.

As they approached the docking bay E1 housing the small vessel that was going to take them down on the surface, One noticed another person inspecting the ship. He was no member of the Crew as far as One knew.

"Excuse me Captain, but who is that?" One said pointing at the stranger.

"That's one of the other members of the Mothership we woke up from his cryosleep. I'll introduce you."

As they approached, the man turned around and waved at them. "Captain! Good to see you. Are we ready?"

"Nearly. I wanted to introduce you to the Xenotechnician that will accompany on our surface mission."

One stepped forward to shake the man's hand. "Pleasure to meet you," he said. "I am Dr. Shape. I'll be assisting you on this mission as a medic and additional hand with repairs or other problems that might come our way." The man's face carried a big smile that showed his excitement for this mission.

"Nice to meet you, but I hope we won't be seeing each other – I'd rather not be needing a medic on our trip," One shifted uneasily while trying to laugh at his own terrible joke.

"Ha! Indeed, I hope so too, but I think the good Captain and the rest of the Crew will ensure our safe return with whatever is waiting for us down there." Shape winked at Jörg who promptly answered the gesture with a pat on the back. "Of course not Dr. Shape. We will all be home for dinner."

"If only dinner wasn't the same boring shit every day!" The

rest of the Crew had caught up to them.

Commander Swayton inspected the ship with narrowed eyes than turned to Jörg. "Everything ready?"

"You tell me," Jörg replied while looking at the Crew.

"As ready as we can be," said Ermis.

"We are set to go," Fèanis added. "The weapons are already on board the ship. I hope we won't have to use them, but better safe than sorry and with sorry I mean fucking dead."

The smile on Jörg's face was gone. "Well then if everything is in order we are ready to leave. The journey to the surface will be short. We'll go through the important things as we descend to the planet. Best of luck, gentlemen. Keep your eyes open and your minds sharp. We will keep this as short and safe as possible."

Schachinger came out of the ship looking at them with a warm smile on his face. "The ship is ready and we're not getting any younger, so I'd say let's hit it!"

As the engine of the small surface transport ship started to hum, One tried to shake of the fear that was suddenly overcoming him.

As his feet touched the ground, One found himself wondering about how long it had been since he stood on an actual planet. How long had he really been asleep? He took a look around and realized he had never felt so far away from home. Although the planet wasn't a total wasteland, hostile to every living thing, it still was necessary for them to wear their environmental suits. Commander Swayton had explained on the way to the surface that this planets air was really thin. It was possible to breath freely for a short time, but there wasn't enough oxygen to survive long-term, which might explain the deserted city.

One couldn't make out a single plant, or even plant-like being. In truth he felt like standing in the middle of a desert. There were mountains all around them, but nothing green caught his eye and as far as he could see there weren't any animals around either. Maybe there were more vital parts of this planet but this one surely wasn't it.

The rest of them had gathered outside the landing ship.

"Alright guys," Jörg's voice rang through his helmet. "We'll split up in two groups. Ermis, Sid and Fèanis will scout the area for any signs of possible threats and make sure the location is actually safe. The Commander, myself and our Xenotechnician will follow the direction of the energy source to see if there is a direct way to it. We will meet up here in an hour for a status report. Dr. Shape will stay with Schachinger at the ship and secure the equipment, as well as being the emergency escape plan in case we need to move out quickly. Any questions?"

"If we find a strip club can we at least get a lap dance?" That was definitely Fèanis' voice. One heard Ermis and Sid giggle into their helmets. The Commander and Jörg ingored the remark completely.

"Just get your shit done and report back in an hour. I expect caution and intelligent behaviour. Did I make myself clear?" the Captain said.

"Yes of course. Stay safe," Ermis replied.

The Commander took a last look around. "Let's get going then. See you later."

They had landed about 10 minutes away from the city itself. The walk gave One some time to take a closer look at his surroundings and the city before him. The ground beneath his feet was hard and dry – cracks were all over the place. The structures in the city seemed to be simple at first, but as they got closer One noticed the very elaborated details. The buildings were very easy on the eye, graceful even. While the houses and buildings back on Gaia had often been nothing more than a rectangle with hard and primitive designs, the structures that lay before him seemed to have no corners at all, but at the same time couldn't be described as round or spherical. It was an amazing sight to behold. Not a big city, but impressive nonetheless.

When they reached the city, a shiver ran down his spine. The city looked completely untouched. No signs of a storm or an explosion, weapon damage or any kind of hostile impact.

"Very strange," Commandor Swayton said as if he read One's thoughts. "No damage anywhere. Not even the slightest hint of it."

"Maybe the outskirts have been left untouched and the actual damage is located at the centre," Jörg added absently. One could nearly hear his wheels spinning.

"I don't know," One said carefully, "the size of the city would indicate that any kind of damage big enough to make the inhabitants leave would be visual throughout the whole city."

The three of them stood silently at the borders of the city. Without a word Jörg shouldered the assault rifle he had brought, and Commandor Swayton followed his example by unlocking the safety of his shotgun. One hesitated. He had been given a standard protection sidearm for this mission but he felt uncomfortable using it. He had chosen science over violence a long time ago, and although he understood that both of them only readied their weapons for self-defence he couldn't bring himself to do the same.

"Don't worry. You don't need to," Jörg said while looking at One's hand on the gun at his side. "We never set out to do harm to anyone or anything, but sadly enough we cannot say the same for the whole universe, right?" One nodded in silent agreement and they continued their way into the city. Commander Swayton stopped and pointed at one of the buildings that was significantly higher than the rest. "We should find some sort of high ground to check if there is a direct way to the signal's location. I didn't see a major temple yet, which is kind of strange given that this is a temple city after all."

They made their way to the building and stopped at the door. "Maybe we should knock," Jörg said.

"You honestly think they locked their doors before disappearing mysteriously?" Swayton replied with a short chuckle.

Jörg answered that by pushing the door open with one hand, "I guess not."

They entered a building filled with strange looking furniture, which for some reason didn't look alien to One. It just reminded him of someone back on Gaia with a weird taste in decorations. All in all there wasn't that much to look at anyway. The decor was really meagre and didn't seem to have any extra kind of artistic purpose. Like the houses and the city itself, everything was in coloured in a pale mix of green and yellow, which didn't make the city stand out much.

They reached a small balcony that allowed them to overlook the city. As One had noticed before, the city was not big at all. Their team could probably explore the entire city in just one day. However, there was something strange about this city. Contrary to most cities on Gaia, this one did not appear to have a city center.

"Interesting," Commander Swayton stated, "there's no temple at the center of the city either."

"Maybe there are more than one, and they are spread across the city," Jörg replied.

"You thought that the energy source is comeing directly from a temple?" One was curious at whether or not they were talking about an energy source from whatever technology was left behind here, or if there was maybe more to it.

"No, we didn't think that the source was located in a temple, but it seems odd for a temple city to have no signs of temples," Commander Swayton answered in a calm and soft tone.

Jörg turned away from the city and said, "You are thinking about structures known to us like they appeared back on Gaia, but we face something totally different. Not all cultures are worshiping something by building cathedrals that are significantly higher and bigger than the rest of the city's buildings."

They made their way back on the street and Commander Swayton pointed in a direction that led them deeper into the city. "Let's try to follow the signal and see if there are any visual obstacles in our way. We have to bring some information back to the rest of the Crew." He unpacked a sensor and started to follow the signal of the energy source.

They went down a few streets but nothing seemed to change. Every turn offered the same view. Empty streets, untouched buildings that revealed nothing about their purpose. Although they carefully watched for any signs of temples or buildings that might give them hints on the location of the energy source, or at least a structure of importance they found nothing.

It seemed as if the whole city was built out of three types of structures, all with the same soft and flawless form, only differing in their height. All had the yellow and green color palette that seemed to somehow merge with the desert surrounding the city.

After some time, Jörg gave the sign to go back and meet up with the others with any clues as to what had happened to the inhabitants of the city or what religion this city was supposed to worship.

"How did you know this is a temple city?" One asked.

"We found the name of the city in our database back on the ship when we scanned the planet. The entry itself was pretty old and hadn't been updated in ages. It said nothing other than this is a temple city, the only settlement on this entire planet. Whoever discovered this city a long time ago didn't bother to give any details about it – or maybe he was forced to delete them. Either way that's how we know about this place." Jörg seemed a little frustrated with not being able to give One a satisfying answer. Maybe that was one of the reasons he and Fèanis argued about the mission, because they actually knew nothing about this place. The city didn't strike One as dangerous, in spite of the lacking knowledge about why this place was abandoned remained unanswered.

They met up with the rest of the Crew back at the ship. The other team couldn't report anything of importance either. It turned out they went through the same experience. Ermis gave them a quick update on the surroundings and stated that there were no visible threats near them, and neither scans nor exploration of the terrain had given a hint on possible physical threats.

As playful as Fèanis and his team had seemed when they set out for their scouting mission there was no sign of even the faintest smile on their faces now. "I think we are ready to track down the energy source. We have been as careful as possible and anything we encounter was not on our radar so I say let's move."

"Fèanis is right," Schachinger added. "You guys have found no indications of danger and I ran a couple of scans from the ship with the same result. Whatever possible threat there might be, we did our best to avoid it and be prepared."

Jörg finally gave the word to set out for the energy source.

"Dr. Shape I am counting on you to stay with the ship and be vigilant to any signs of us being in a hasty return from whatever we might find. We are counting on you."

Shape looked at the Captain with a straight face and gave him a short salute. "Will do. Take care, all of you. I will await your return."

One noticed something as he watched the Crew move into the city – all six of them were moving and acting as one unit, as if they were of one mind. Maybe it was due the fact that they had known each other for such a long time, but One couldn't help but think that with all the joking and playful banter every single member of the Crew was as focused as they could possibly be, ready for everything. They all knew their task and One could catch glimpses of the real people behind the faces he had seen in the briefing room back on the ship. They cared for each other and every turn they took, every street they encountered, they all watched out for each other, keeping One in their middle as if to shield him from unseen enemies. He felt as safe as the situation allowed, but maybe more importantly he felt ensured in his decision to join the Mothership and its cause. These people were working together to make something happen that was greater than themselves or any negative feelings and petty arguments.

They had been moving towards the signal for about an hour when they suddenly stood in front of a large crater.

At first One thought they had finally found the reason for abandonment of the city, because at a first glance it seemed the crater was the result of a hostile impact, but after a few moments he realized it was something else. Although it didn't appear to be manmade, One suspected that the city had been built around the crater, making the crater itself the centre of the city. Structures and buildings on the inside slopes of the crater indicated this.

"Well, that explains why we failed to locate the centre of the city. Seems like important things are built down, not up." Fèanis stood at the rim of the crater, looking down at the large hole in the ground.

"Look, there," Swayton pointed at the middle of the crater, where One could make out a large building, perhaps the biggest they had seen yet. "All the information from our instruments seems to point us towards that building. Whatever it is, we'll find our energy source there."

One noticed a small path leading down to the bottom of the huge crater. Jörg seemed to have noticed it too because he started to move in its direction.

"Ok guys," he said with a commanding voice. "We take this path down to the center. Stay focused and look out for any kind of trouble. Whatever is down there, we can't be too careful. Understood?"

They moved down the slope, passing bigger and bigger buildings as they moved towards the centre. Although the size of the buildings changed significantly, the architecture was the same as they had seen in the rest of the city. The path led them in large circles around the crater, spiralling down towards the bottom.

One couldn't make out how much time passed during their journey to the bottom. It could have been hours or just 10 minutes. Nobody said a word and as they moved in silence, checking every building on the way. The group grew more and more tense. Like the buildings they had encountered in the rest of the city, the crater buildings held no clue of the events that had led to the abandonment of the city. No signs of a fight, no signs of inhabitants. Everything seemed like people had been here just a few days ago.

They stopped when they reached the building at the centre. A huge dome stood before them – a dome with a distinctly different architecture and color than all other buildings. The most significant difference was the material it was made of. Although it appeared to be stone, it was not like anything

One had seen so far. It was as black as space itself and seemed darker than the deepest night. At first he thought it was meteorite, but as he got closer and touched the wall of the building, he noticed that the surface felt nothing like stone at all, but closely resembled the touch of wood even though there visually it looked nothing like it.

"Amazing," Commander Swayton touched the wall beside One, "what kind of material is this?'

"I have no idea," One could only shrug uncomfortably. He wasn't really thrilled like he used to be, when encountering such extraordinary things. The whole city seemed just wrong to him.

"We should take samples and take a look at it back on the ship," Jörg said as he stood behind them and looked concerned, "but first let's take a look at the inside. Our top priority is to find the energy source."

With a silent nod Commander Swayton turned away from the wall. "At least we don't have to search for a way in," he said while looking straight at the large arc-like entrance to the building. "I guess it was an open temple, freely accessible to all citizens. '

Schachinger carefully took a look around the entrance and peeked inside. "Let's find ourselves an energy source then, shall we?'

As they entered the temple they had to activate their low-light vision. It was as if they had walked into the night. Even with their goggles on it was hard to make out anything in the large, empty space.

"Over there! Look!" Sid moved towards a dim and very distant shimmer that was hard to concentrate on. They followed Sid and as they got closer One realised that their goal was the centre of the dome. It had already seemed enormous from the outside, but felt even bigger now they were inside.

It appeared as if there was only one large chamber, the one they were in right now. No sign of any kind of furniture. As they got closer to the centre, they could make out a small podium in the middle of the dome. It was simple, not very high and not big at all. Compared to the size of the dome it actually seemed ridiculously small. It was not the podium itself that drew their attention, it was the object placed on it.

Through a small hole in the dome a faint ray of light illuminated a black object on the podium. Its form was bizarre and unlike anything One had seen before. It appeared to be predominantly round, but there were at least two angles he could make out. It was strange in every kind of way. Ornaments graced its surface, but neither did they make any kind of sense to him nor could he tell their actual colour. The object seemed to absorb the darkness around him, somehow it was even darker than the dome that surrounded them.

There was no sign of a barrier around the podium – no warning signs. The object seemed free for the taking.

"Is it just me or does it strike anyone else as suspicious that there is a relict on a podium in the middle of a deserted temple city, in the middle of nowhere without any kind of defence mechanisms or guards to watch over it?" Fèanis remarked, with a voice was more than tense. "Free for the taking it might be. But I do not trust this thing. Not even one bit."

"I agree," Swayton said. "With everything we did encounter

or actually did not encounter, I am not sure it is wise to take whatever this object might be."

Jörg stepped closer. "It's definitely the source of energy we have been looking for. That much is clear." He looked at his sensors as if to make sure he was really correct.

"Object in the middle of an abandoned town. Not a living soul here and no objects of value to be found but this thing. Anyone could have taken it and yet no one did. Yeah, that does indeed sound like a very bad idea." Ermis added while he moved around the object and shook his head. "Whatever this is. It is bad news. I can tell you that much."

One barely heard the last sentence and the discussion about the nature of the object faded into a dull rumbling. One did not listen. He did not care. All he was interested in was the relic on the podium. Its form, its colour, the strange ornaments, everything was so fascinating. If only he could study it on the ship. Scan it and do experiments on it. Surely he could make a valuable source of power for the mothership. The inhabitants of this city couldn't release the relic's full potential. They had probably been simple and primitive folk who couldn't use the object for anything else than worshiping. Perhaps they had thought of it as some sort of god – the centre of a primitive culture.

He had to study this object, had to explore its secrets, its value – its power. He had to have it. It seemed more important to him each passing second. His instincts as a scientist told him to study this object. It was of utter importance. For science. For the Mothership.

"We need to take this back to the ship. I need to study this object. I am sure I can turn this into a most valuable power source for our mission!"

The discussion between the members of the Crew stopped abruptly.

Schachinger looked at him. "What?'

"We definitely found what we were looking for. This object is very valuable to us. If you allow me to bring it onto the ship I can prove it to you!"

"Why do you think it is a good idea to bring this relic on board the ship? Even if it is valuable, it's clearly dangerous and we don't know what it can do!" Fèanis' raised his voice. He was tense and did not seem to be happy at One's suggestion. "Look around you. Do these surroundings strike you as very secure and safe? Do you feel comfortable in deserted cities!?"

"That's enough, Fèanis," Jörg said with a harsh tone. "We brought a Xenotechnician for a reason. I share your points of concern, but we have to consider all possibilities. So tell me, how can we be sure, this isn't a fatal mistake?" he asked One.

"We can never be completely sure. If this object would be dangerous, we would clearly have noticed by now. I mean, look at it! It's fascinating and clearly this city was some simpler religious cult that couldn't use this relic's power to its full potential." He stepped towards the relic and touched it. He could hear the others breathe in sharply. Nothing happened. "See? Nothing. It is not dangerous and just because whoever left it here could not awaken its potential doesn't mean we should leave it here as well. We need the energy source for our travels, right? For our mission? Why make all this effort if we're just leaving it here? You brought me here to tell you more about objects we find and give you my scientific opinion. Well, my opinion is: we should take it with us!"

They all looked at him, and for a short moment One was sure he had overstepped his boundaries. But he didn't care, he simply had to have this object for his research. It was vital – he needed it!

"Very well," Jörg didn't sound too certain, but he seemed to have considered One's words. "We take it with us and you can start your experiments and research as soon as we get back to the ship. But listen to me. If we see anything dangerous or suspicious regarding this relic, we will get rid of it as soon as possible."

"Understood," One tried to hide is excitement.

"Ok guys. Let's get this thing out of here," Commander Swayton said as started to prepare one of the carriages they had brought alon. Fèanis, Sid and Ermis seemed concerned, and Schachinger looked even more troubled, but they followed their orders and started preparing the object for transportation back to the ship. One was smiling. He was looking forward to whatever he would discover. It surely marked the beginning of a grand scientific adventure.

The way back to the ship was quiet. As they got back to the ship, a Dr. Shape greeted them. He didn't comment their finding, which was odd and One was mildly irritated for a moment. Even though he only knew Dr. Shape very briefly, this did not fit his character. One dismissed his thoughts as exhaustion. He was clearly just overreacting.

The relic – it was all his fault. His body was shaking as the cameras silently judged him. Everything was silent. He heard nothing but his own breathing. Shallow and rapid.

I can't be – this is all my fault!

He had persuaded them to bring the relic on board, to let him study it and reveal the secrets hidden beneath the surface. Only that there had been no secrets, no hidden scientific treasure. The relic had turned out to be their demise.

His memories of the time after the mission were still blurry, but now One knew what had happened. He knew what he became after they got back to the ship. Obsession had taken over, obsession with the relic, with its hidden purpose, with its unknown nature. He had lost himself in studies, experiments. Days and nights without eating or sleeping, without talking to any other member of the Crew. Just him and the relic, just his experiments. That thing had been the centre of his thoughts, like the eye of a storm, surrounded by the chaos of his mind, destroying every bit of sanity in its way.

He remembered the experiments, the insane amount of energy he had applied to the relic. He had tried to energize it with more and more energy every day. It got completely out of hand. The Crew eventually had to detain him so he could get some rest, but One snuck back in, continuing his experiments. No matter how much energy he had applied, the relic had absorbed it all like a dry sponge absorbs water. It had driven him to insanity. An increasing amount of resources had been wasted by him. In the end he got carried away to a point where he tried to change the course of the ship to charge the relic near a red giant. That's when they locked him away again, sent him back to his cryosleep. It had been for their protection and for his own.

As One sat on the floor his chest felt so heavy. The intensity of his shame was so strong that he couldn't breathe. He was paralyzed by the guilt he felt. It was his fault. He had doomed the Mothership. He had doomed the Crew. Not only had he endangered the mission, he was likely the reason for its failure. He was the reason this journey had come to an end and they were all going to die somewhere in the depths of space.

You are not dead yet. You know the problem. You know what to do.

Yes, he knew what to do, but just not how he was supposed to do it. He had to get to the relic. If he died on this ship he had to try at least, try to right his wrongs, make up for his mistakes.

You owe it to them.

Slowly, and with shaking knees, he got up and looked at the closed bulkhead. He took a few steps toward it and then straightened up. This was where he had to take a stand.

It's either sink or swim... and I am not ready to sink yet.

With every spark of energy that was left in his body he threw himself at the bulkhead and tried to open it with the sheer power of his muscles. At first his arms burned up with pain like they were about to snap like twigs, but One ignored it. All he thought about was how he had lost himself to his obsession, how his egoistic behaviour had put others at risk, how his actions had nearly cost them everything and most likely would kill them all. The guilt ran through his body like a poison, and when it nearly became unbearable he screamed out in agony mobilizing the last bit of strength in an outburst of rage. The bulkhead uncoiled violently and he nearly fell on his back, surprised by its sudden motion.

Exhausted One stood in front of the open bulkhead. There

was his way. He wasn't sure whether he'd find his way back to the Dante Tray, grim determination took over and without hesitation he gathered his things and left the small space that had witnessed the return of his memory and the tip of his emotional ruin.

Sink or swim.

SIX

LIGHTBEARER

Time is a very strange thing. Although there are exact methods of measurement for different units and categories, as well as a very detailed description on the phenomenon of time itself, there is still a very elaborate mystery to the character of time. Hours can turn into days, while days can turn into mere minutes, and a beautiful evening can pass in what seems a blink of an eye. The fact that you can experience time that has been measured as exactly a minute, for subjectively much longer can drive you insane, as much as it can be a blessing in moments of danger. Moments that otherwise might have passed by as seconds can stretch out to be half an hour if your life depends on it. That gives the human mind the ability – and the curse – to experience time in as many different ways as there are human minds. If we are willing to accept this vague characteristic of time, we can maybe begin to grasp the horrifying experience of a person with mental illness who appears to have come back from years of suffering, although we just left them alone for just a few hours."

Dr. Hora Aetas, The Last Enemy Of Humanity's Golden Age. Time and Mental Illness, Archives of the Gaian Institute of Mind Studies, Book XVII, Chapter 6, Page 450

"Storage Unit No. 32," One read on the sign next to the open door. He had no idea why he had just read it out loud. He knew that sign already. He had passed it about 4 times now. The open door didn't surprise him anymore either. After all he had been the one to open it. As useful as the storage room had been in the beginning, it turned out to be the trademark of a curse now.

When he first came by the storage unit he had been full of joy, because he had finally escaped the small ladder and bulkhead filled trays the shapeshifter had led him into. He had been so happy to see a different kind of surrounding that he didn't even mind the absolute lack of power in this part of the ship. He didn't even mind the gravity relays failing randomly, sending silently floating storage boxes, chairs and cases back to the floor with a thundering sound that echoed terribly in the ship.

However, now, all those things started to wear him down. The only source of light came from the flashlight he held in his hand and the small lights from his suit. His eyes had adapted to the darkness that surrounded him, but his mind began to slowly fade every minute he wandered the empty corridors.

What first had seemed as a way out had now become a labyrinth. He remembered a story he had read back on Gaia. It was a tale of an ancient civilisation long gone. It spoke of a king that tried to trick a god, so his wife was struck with a curse which damned her to give birth to a horrible creature that was half man and half animal. They build a labyrinth in which they sacrificed younglings and virgins to feed the beast.

One stopped and rested his head against the wall.

A beast. That is all that's missing in this nightmare.

A loud metallic sound echoed through the hallway as his helmet met the cold steel of the wall. A labyrinth. That was exactly what it felt like. Although he was not quite sure how long exactly he had been in this section of the ship, One felt like he had known this storage room for his entire life.

Time for another round in my labyrinth. Maybe I am the beast?

Slowly he made his way down the hallway again. He tried to avoid everything that seemed slightly familiar, because he didn't want to end up at his storage room again. It was a hard task to even be able to see what was in front and around him. The lights from his suit illuminated just a small area. The rest were shadows and darkness. His mind had been very challenged by the task not to imagine human figures in every corner. Many times he had crossed sections were an energy barrier had been the only thing that separated him from the deadly cold of the space. The light of the barrier and his flashlights had given him spooky visions of his own silhouette. After all this time alone and in the darkness, even his scientific trained mind began to wander and imagine things that weren't there. More than one time he had jumped at the sight of a shadow figure awaiting him at the end of a hallway.

He took another turn. The hallway seemed familiar and at the same time he couldn't make out anything he had seen before.

I feel like a blind man stumbling through a labyrinth. At this point I would be happy if the beast showed up and ate me.

Another energy barrier. He could see the endless depth of space before him. The stars shining bright. His own light and the light from the barrier touched and formed scary shadows along the hallway. His feet left the ground. He was floating.

Another gravity relay that stopped functioning. How long till they all collapse?

As One continued through the hallway the silence terrified him the most. The never ending silence. The only sounds he heard came from himself. His breathing was the only constant sound he could make out. From time to time he heard a distant noise when a gravity relay started to work again and send all the floating things smashing back to the ground. In the beginning it had just been an annoying sound that made him jump. Now it began to scare him. It felt like the beast was knocking. Waiting until someone let it in.

Am I going insane?

It was a hard question to answer. Reality clearly started to fade. He had been alone in this darkness for too long. He already had no idea where he was anymore. Although One had tried to remember the turns and hallways he took, the doors he had passed, he still had no clue of this section's structure. His mind couldn't focus anymore and drifted more and more into useless thoughts and illusions. Memories from his time on Gaia and stories he had been told.

How did the story of the beast and the labyrinth end? Didn't they slay the beast?

He couldn't remember. It was of no use anyway. Remembering wouldn't get him out of this mess. But then again, what would?

He made another turn. Another hallway, but at the end was something unusual. A person. He could clearly see someone standing there. Looking at him. One hurried, nearly running.

There was someone else down here, someone who could help him. He started to run – excitement started to take over. Finally, he was not alone. That stranger could help him get out of here.

As he finally reached the stranger he abruptly stopped. The only thing staring back at him was his own reflection. He stood in front of what seemed to be a giant mirror. Although made out of metal it reflected its surroundings clearly. He could make out every detail in its surrounding and the closer he got the bigger he appeared.

He definitely hadn't been here before – not that it mattered, this was just another dead end. He had been tricked by another illusion of the labyrinth. He screamed out in anger.

He called out the names of the Crew, called out for the shapeshifter, but no one answered. The silence mocked his ridiculous attempts of escape once more by responding with nothingness. The labyrinth had its iron grip on him and was not willing to let him go.

Why is this giant metal mirror here anyway? What is the point of putting it at the end of some random hallway? They must've put it here just to mock me. The Crew. It's probably just a game to them... Maybe it is some test? Are they testing me? Or is this the last trick of the shapeshifter? Nothing makes sense anymore.

One stumbled away from the giant mirror and looked around. In the distance he could hear the crates and boxes of the storage room crushing down on the floor again.

I am going insane. I can't do this anymore.

How long has he been here? What day was it? Was there even a point in trying to save this ship or was everything lost already?

Maybe the Crew was dead. He'd probably taken to long.

I have failed the Crew.

He looked back at his reflection in the giant mirror. He looked tired, exhausted, beaten. Lost.

Whoever put that mirror here had known it would be his ending. The last joke on his journey to failure. It seemed like an eternity since he had woken up in his cryocell. As far as One was concerned he should have remained in his slumber, remained on Gaia, and remained ignorant to everything. What good does an open mind do you, if everything around you is either dying or destroyed?

It seems like I finally found the beast.

His own image staring back at him in silent agreement. The beast of the labyrinth. The failure of the ship and the disappointment of the Crew.

He could have stood there for a century. His brain mind wandered and visited old places, old memories from the time when nothing had bothered him, back in the days when he had been unaware of everything.

Still, he knew he had to go back. There had to be another route to get to where he wanted to go, but One had a hard time remembering what he was looking for and where it was he wanted to go. Nothing really seemed to matter.

I will never leave this labyrinth. I am trapped here. I cannot escape. I cannot get out. I cannot...

There was a sound behind him. It started as a very distant whisper, but as it grew louder and more intense it started to fill the empty space around One. The silence was pushed away by what seemed to be some sort of hissing, like wind blowing through a tiny hole in the wall.

Is the ship finally falling apart? At least that would put an end to this nightmare...

One forced himself to turn around and look for the origin of the sound. He didn't have to look very far.

Right behind him a compressed air pump had suddenly started to work. One of the security doors that had been closed until now suddenly stood open. He hadn't done anything to it, so maybe it was another failing system that started to open doors. Carefully One stepped towards the door to find out what was behind it.

One saw a very long and big hallway in front of him. It led straight ahead, no turns, no other doors. At the end of the hallway was a light. Considering his other option, of slowly going insane starting at himself in the mirror, he entered the newly opened hallway. As he passed the doorway he noticed a sign, "Please check your gear for damage in the monitoring mirror to your right". One gave the mirror another glance, slowly shaking his head over his own naïve stupidity.

The hallway seemed endless, but the gravity relay seems to work properly. As he got closer to the source of the light at the end of the hallway, he started to realize that this time he wasn't confronted with another illusion. This was real. Whatever it was – it was real.

At the end of the corridor was a maximum security door. He turned off his flashlights since the door itself had multiple lights installed. As One came closer to the door, it opened unprompted to a large white room.

He entered, squinting to protect his eyes from the bright white light filling the room. The light still hurt his eyes, but slowly he started to adapt to the unusual brightness. After all his time in the darkness of the corridors of the ship, he was very happy about a fully functioning environment. He took a look around to find out where he found himself.

The room was clinically tidy and there wasn't one spot that seemed like it hadn't been cleaned just a few minutes ago. There were working stations everywhere. One walked around slowly, walking from computer to computer. They all seemed ready for work, like everything had been prepared for his arrival.

He stopped in front of the only active screen, displaying a lot of data streams and images. Everything seemed to run automatically. One stepped a little closer and suddenly all the data streams seemed to come together like rivers pouring into an ocean. In front of him an image started to appear. It was a form he knew and as soon as he recognized it, it began to frighten him. Not only did he know what was in the image before him, he knew it as well as the back of his own hand – it was the relic.

Before his eyes, the image of the relic came to life. It was as he had remembered it. Every little detail was there – every single part of its surface. Next to the image of the relic itself, One could make out data streams that were showing analysis about the condition of the relic as well as the molecular consistency and energy dynamics inside of it. One was familiar with the majority of data displayed on the screen, because they were based on his research and experiments, but something was off. The data streams and analysis were much more elaborate and advanced than his own before his research had been interrupted. Someone must have continued his research after they had put him back in his cryocell. But who? It couldn't have been the Crew – even with all their skills, they weren't able to continue his studies on such a high level of scientific proficiency. There had to be someone else.

Who could have done this?

If that person, whoever they were, was still alive, maybe One could finally get some desperately needed help on his mission. That person could help him save this ship if it wasn't already too late.

One took off his protective gear and drank his last liquid rations. He sat down at one of the working stations.

Let's see who this person is.

With a simple touch the working station came to life.

Remarkable. The whole ship is falling apart but this research station seems like it hasn't been touched at all.

He didn't complain. One was happy about the fact that at least one time something on the ship still worked and he could try to find a way forward instead of blindly going in circles.

He checked the research logs, but found nothing other than his own entries and notes.

Whoever continued my work did not follow the standard procedure. Interesting.

One was so engrossed in his thoughts that he nearly missed a small but very important detail. His own name. It seemed so familiar to him on screen, he hadn't even realized it. "One, M.A.I., Chief Xenotechnician, Crew Status: Level 1 confidant."

Without knowing, I instantly picked the same name as I did when we left earth.

He remembered the day he chose his new name. Every new member had the chance to either change his name or keep the old one. One had chosen a new name, because he wanted to be one of the many people to help building a new future, a better future. A future where minds aren't closed on purpose but open for the right reasons. He was One. One of many to accomplish something greater than himself, just like the Crew they were following into the depths space. At the same time he had chosen this name because he wanted to be one with the divinity of the universe and space, the SPARK that infused the new era of humanity. He wanted to be one with the great ideas that had made humanity become more than just living beings fighting for their own survival.

It felt good to finally see his name again and to know what its purpose was; his own purpose for that matter. It gave him new confidence. For the first time since ages a smile came across his lips. Maybe all wasn't lost.

One had searched for some time now, but still found no clue about the person continuing his research. There was nothing to be found in either the personal files, catalogues of the ship nor the logs from the various research stations. It was always his own name that appeared as the last working member concerning the research of the relic. It all led to the same conclusion: someone must have continued the research off the grid. As impossible as it appeared, since cameras monitored the relic, it was the only explanation.

Suddenly, he heard the humming sound of another working station coming to life. One turned around to see which one. Directly opposite of him another screen had switched on. It showed the complete plan of the ship. One got up from his workstation and walked over.

The whole Mothership with all its structures, levels and sections was displayed on the screen. As One stepped closer, a specific section of the ship suddenly was highlighted red and enlarged till he could make out a single room with a lonely figure standing in front of a workstation.

That's me. That is my location!

The workstation zoomed out and highlighted a route that led to a section just underneath the lab he was in right now. Next to it the name of the section itself popped up. Section 66.

S-66. Why does that sound so familiar? Of course – that's where the relic is. In S-66!

Another screen came to life to his left and displayed a hologram with graphs of energy dynamics. Right next to it was a small model of an energy stream showing the position of the Mothership. The Mothership was close to the Spark nebula, the remains of a super nova which was still wearing out at the centre. Below the image of the spark nebula it read "Xibalba" and One finally started to realize the plan.

They want to recharge the ship's core and energy reserves by aspirating the remaining radiation of the nebular, converting it into a usable energy to fuel the ship.

As soon as One realized the purpose of the ships location, the on-screen graphs changed and displayed the familiar energy signals of the relic next to the one's from the ship itself.

Wait – it appears that the relic absorbed the energy from the nebula. Of course! Of course it can absorb it. It's using the ship's core as an energy converter and the ship itself as a funnel-medium to absorb all the energy. No wonder the on-board system's collapsed. The amount of raw energy taken in is enough to make the entire ship blow up! It's a miracle I am still alive and the ship hasn't burnt up. That's definitely why the systems all shut down. They prevented the ship from collapsing entirely.

One knew what he had to do. He would need to perform a slingshot-like manoeuvre to throw the relic into the nebulas' centre and away from the ship.

The Crew needs to get the systems online as fast as possible to get us out of here or the reaction of the nebula's core and the relic will destroy us all.

It was a very risky plan. A single mistake and they would end up dead.

One got back to his gear. His water rations were gone and only a few energy bars remained. As he looked back at the route towards section 66, a single room was highlighted green. It was a storage room. One walked over to the workstation and typed "thx Crew" into the terminal window.

Although it had seemed like they had abandoned him, in the end they came through and saved him again. It was a comforting thought to know that they were still out there, trying their best to keep him alive and going on his mission.

As he made his way towards the exit that would lead him to section 66 he saw that someone had answered his message. He froze in front of the screen as he read the message, "Not Crew – Ghost.exe"

It had not been the Crew who had shown him the way. It had been the ship itself.

SEVEN

SUPERNOVA SUNBATHING

As One stood in front of what was supposed to be storage unit S-66 there were two emotions running through his body.

One of them was excitement. He had reached his destination and he definitely knew what the problem was.

Once you know what the problem is, you can easily solve it. At least that is what science taught me.

He been wandering around the ship for so long that it felt good to finally have a destination.

At the same time, One was terrified. What he saw made his knees weak, his stomach twist and sent his mind spinning.

This part should have been spared by the massive destruction that befell the rest of the Mothership, but this wasn't the case at all. One looked at a much more complex kind of destruction than he had seen before. This wasn't just regular damage from shockwaves and energy overloads. It seemed like every spark of energy had been drained completely form this section.

No light was working properly, no electrical component was intact. He could deal with this lack of energy as he had done before, but what he was looking at would not be that easy to overcome.

The entrance to the storage unit was covered and sealed by something that looked like the roots from a tree. However, somehow it didn't look biological. As he stood in front of the strange structure that was covering the door he tried to make out any signs of organic tissues, but what he found was distinctly not organic. He leaned in on the strange structure and poked it. Nothing happened. One could make out a very weak pulse though. It ran through the whole structure and made it look like some sort of vein, but only once you knew the pulse was even there.

What are you? That colour... It seems like it has none. It appears as black as night but at the same time...

"Fuck."

Although he whispered it, he could feel its echo running through every single empty corridor on the ship as he realised what kind of material he was looking at.

Of course! Why else would this part of the ship be drained like a used up battery. Only one material I ever saw comes close to this thing...

It was the same material as the relic.

Although he couldn't understand how, he was sure that he was looking at a part of the relic, an extension of it. He knew it. He knew the material, the structure that eluded every explanation.

It appears to have grown, but how and how much?

There was only one way to find out. No matter what was

awaiting him inside the storage unit there was certainly no way back now.

He grabbed the arc welder from his kit and took a deep breath.

I hope this will work.

It was surprisingly easy to cut through the structure. It didn't take One long to free the door and the console next to it. As soon as the structure came off the console started to come to life, energy suddenly pouring through it again.

It seems to absorb every last drop the energy around it and fed to whatever this thing really is. It is to energy what a sponge is to water.

He opened the door and stepped into what seemed like a vision from hell itself.

Dark was not the word for the sheer blackness in front of him. Walls, doors, consoles and screens, everything was covered by the strange vein-like structures. There was no sound to hear but a very distant buzzing. The farther One got into the storage unit the more he realized that the buzzing was not continuous but followed a sort of rhythmic pattern.

It is like heart beat... it's almost as if it is... alive?!

Although he was terrified to his very core of his being, One kept pushing on. As he made his way through he cut down more and more parts of the structure, only to find it growing back almost as fast as he could cut it down.

Finally he stood in front of the door sealing the chamber where the relic was kept.

It ends now. I will finish this.

He freed the door and stepped into the large room holding the relic and all he could do was stand in awe.

Holy mother of...

In front of him was not the small, chest-like object they had brought back from their mission, but a huge monstrosity that was covering the entire room. Every electronic device had been swallowed by the huge mass of blackness. The buzzing grew so loud One had to cover his ears. Like a huge deformed heart, the relic sat there, pulsing, waiting.

It is huge, but it's weak. There is not enough energy left in this section of the ship. That must be why it is spreading. Now is my chance!

He confidently took a step towards the relic and started his arc welder. At first it seemed to work just as well as it had with the vein-like structures and One felt a smile crossing his face when suddenly a very intense burst of energy seemed to explode right in front of him, throwing him across the room. The impact drove the air out of his lungs. Suddenly he was fighting to stay conscious.

When he got back to his feet, he on some scanning equipment he had brought. Unlike its veins, the relic itself had some sort of protective cover that shielded it from the damage. It seemed to absorb the incoming damage only to reflect it moments later. He wouldn't be able to weld his way through that monstrosity. He had to do something different.

I have to get rid of it! But how?

One looked around, hoping he could find some clues on how to deal with the relic, but nothing he saw triggered a useful idea. He damaged of a vein in anger, watching it fall to the ground and losing its grip and slowly dying on the floor.

If I could just cut it off from the ship somehow... wait... that might be it!

He could cut off this entire section of the ship. That would solve the problem of the energy drain and at the same time separate the relic form this Mothership!

The gravity of the nebula will suck it in and we could start the engine again! Yes — that's it!

One ran out of the room to make his way towards the section control that would enable him to disconnect the storage unit form the rest of the ship. It was a hard fight through the relic-covered hallways. It almost seemed like the relic knew his plan and wanted to stop him. The veins grew faster and more persistent. When he finally reached the section control, One was covered in sweat and his welder was running hot. He could feel that he did not have much time left.

He worked for what seemed like an eternity to rid the section control of the energy-draining veins, and he was close to giving up when he finally saw one console come to life. Multiple screens followed and slowly the whole room lit up.

One felt relieved and quickly sat behind the main controls and started to initialize the sequence that would undock the storage unit from the rest of the ship. After a few minutes of preparation, everything was set and he initialized the undocking sequence. He could hear a rumbling noise, and watching on the screens he could see one attachment after another go down, support holdings break and wires tear. The whole section shook and the rumbling noise grew louder as One slowly backed towards a wall and sat down to rest his body against the wall of the ship.

It's over — I have done it!

One could feel a final wave of relief washing over him as he saw storage unit S-66 drifting towards the Xibalba's nebula on the monitors in the room. It was over. He slumped down and rested his eyes.

What woke him up wasn't the well-earned silence of a victory. It the furious shaking of a situation gone very wrong. One knew the moment he got to his feet that something was not right. Something had not gone as planned. The whole ship shook.

He stumbled towards the consoles to check on the situation. He hadn't slept for long because the storage unit was still close to the ship, drifting towards the nebula. Waves of energy lashed out at the Mothership, and they came from the nearby unit S-66.

He realized the mistake he had made. The relic hadn't been dangerous before because there had not been enough energy. There certainly was now. The relic had come to life.

Wave after wave hit the ship. By itself, the waves were weak and there wasn't much damage to the ship, but One knew that it was only a matter of time before the Mothership would suffer the full power of the relic.

I have no idea what this thing is really capable of. How could I have missed this!?

The sensor readings confirmed what he already knew by now. The relic fed on the energy of the nebula. He had been so eager to get rid of the relic, so proud that he had figured out a way that he forgot to think his plan through. He was sure that this time it would be their doom. The nebula would energize the relic up to a point where its powers would be greater than anything anyone had experienced before.

I have doomed us all.

He started to cry. His final attempt to solve the situation he was responsible for was the nail in his coffin.

I have killed the Crew. I have killed us all. Unless...

It was not over yet. There was still time. He could still make it right.

There has to be a way out. Think!

There was not enough energy to get the tractor beams working, and the weapon systems could only be accessed by the Crew and there was no way of reaching them right now.

I can't let it end like this! I need to get the relic out of the nebula... I need a ship – a small shuttle. If I time my approach correctly I can get the relic back to the ship without getting hit by one of these waves.

It was a long shot, but it was all he got. There was no time for hesitation. It was risky, but if he died during this mission he would die knowing he tried everything and didn't just give up and perish in self-pity.

It took him a while to get to the shuttle bay. It was not easy getting through the sections of the ship with the emergency lockdown activated in many parts of the ship. His determination gave him the speed and the strength to reach the shuttle bay in time and see his mission through. He knew it. This was it.

Sink or swim.

As he entered the shuttle bay, the scenery of destruction that lay before him made him stop for a second. The damage that had been done since he had last been here was intense.

Everywhere he looked there were destroyed ships, broken wings, smashed shuttle viewports.

How am I supposed to find a shuttle in this devastation?

He started checking all the vessels that seemed intact, only to find their electronics fried or hulls breached.

After he checked on two destroyed transporters, he found on that was miraculously still intact. Heavily armoured, with strong shields and a claw arm on top. As he started the ships systems to see if they were still functioning, he took a look around. His eye caught the name of the ship written on the top of the cockpit, "Daedalus."

Isn't that based on Daedalus, a figurine of Greek mythology? Yeah... he appears at the court of King Minos in the story of the Labyrinth.

He found himself smiling at the strange sense of irony as the systems started and the ship readied itself for take-off.

The Daedalus slowly inched towards what had been section S-66 of the Mothership. The nebular grew brighter as he got closer to S-66. One used the ship's external arm to cut into S-66, when suddenly the Daedalus' energy readings showed that the next wave was about to start.

Come on – I can make it!

He ripped apart bulkheads and continued cutting – the Daedalus didn't fool around and forced its way through debris, walls, doors and corridors with relative ease.

The energy readings went off the chart when he finally made it to the relic. It was a hard fight to get the relic out of its chamber, where it had nested like an electronic brood mother.

The Daedalus took a lot of damage trying to force the relic out, but in the end he was successful.

With a ticking time bomb held out in front of him, One set course for the Mothership, knowing it was only a matter of time before the next wave would hit. The sensors showed slightly diminishing energy levels, but dangerous nonetheless.

A deep tone suddenly rose from the inside of the Daedalus and One could barely get his helmet on in time, as he realized the energy wave was ripping the outer hull of the ship apart, punching holes into the ship. The shields went down and the reactor core died. One was now drifting through space with a dead ship around him, the relic in front of him and the Mothership so close but still too far away. The Daedalus was off course, so momentum wouldn't get him to the Mothership. He wouldn't reach it doing nothing.

There was only one option. He knew what it was, but the realisation made his legs shake. He would have to space dive.

One opened the emergency hatch and crawled out of the ship, carefully moving to the front of the ship where the relic was. When he reached the nose he stopped. One would have to make a huge, will timed and aligned jump, grab the relic and avoid the debris still floating between him and the Mothership to float back into the hanger like a dead fish in the water.

Everything or nothing. All in.

He jumped.

It felt like it had taken an eternity to reach the relic, which One grabbed with shaking hands. He continued to float through the endless dark space between the Daedalus and the Mothership. Clutching the relic tight to his chest, hands shaking, face sweating behind the closed off helmet he could do nothing but drift in space, hoping that he would be on time and on course – that it would be enough.

This is how I am going to die, isn't it?

One closed his eyes and gripped the relic tighter. Maybe he would make it, maybe not. He didn't dare to look. It was not in his power anymore. He did all he could and gave everything he had. What more could anyone want from him?

Heavily breathing he opened his eyes just a little bit to see if there was any chance to reach the hanger at all... The image he saw made him burst into tears and smile at the same time. Just as he had opened his eyes again he was floating through the big gates of the hanger.

He made it.

Carrying pure destruction in his arms.

EIGHT

ASCENSION

He looked down at the force of destruction that was resting in his arms. It looked peaceful, like the eye of a storm. He could still feel it pulsing or at least imagined that he could. He wasn't certain. All he knew was that he had to get rid of it. It was literally in his hands now to right the wrongs and get the Mothership back on track. Save the Crew. Save the ship. Save so many lives that unknowingly depended on him. He had to succeed.

One frantically checked if his equipment was still there. He had lost some of the equipment along the way, but luckily his scanner and data recorder were still there. He quickly turned them on and pointed everything towards the relic. There had to be something that he had missed. Something didn't add up and there had to be an explanation for that.

I have to go back all the way to the moment we found this relic. There has to be something I didn't see, a mistake I made... the last piece of this puzzle.

One stared at the screens of both devices as they retrieved

all data he had on the relic and the planet it came from. He was still in the hanger while the data was loading, and looked around to find a good spot to set up his scanners for further analysis. He knew time was short. He knew he had to solve this one last mystery soon, or it had all been for nothing. Now was the time to unravel the last of its secrets. Now was the time for all of his studies and devotion to come together and pay off. Or he would die – they all would die.

He set up in one of the damaged shuttles. The scanners were working, the displays flashing with analysed data, his eyes frantically going over every little detail from their mission. He looked at the video footage of the city and read the reports and analyses. More and more he felt like he was there again – back in the temple city on Bashara.

What did I miss? What detail got lost in all of this?

A voice from the video footage suddenly caught his attention. "Seems like there were some sort of subcontinents deeper within the planets core that somehow shielded toxic matter from reaching the surface." It was his own voice. "Apparently this planet has always been sort of wild and unpredictable but it should never have been as bad as this. The topographic tracings would have been different."

He was listening to his own observations and research. It had never struck him as important, but somehow it stood out this time. What was so important about this? It seemed the relic had somehow polluted the planet and killed every living human being.

Then why wasn't there any sign of destruction on the planet? Everything was intact, but now the ship is being torn apart by its power. It doesn't make sense...

A sudden thought struck him. What if the relic never was asleep? What if it had been awake the whole time while it was on the planet?

Why did it not destroy the city like its destroying the ship?!

One heard himself on the voice logs again, "...type of energy... not traceable... seems like it is gone..." but he wasn't listening anymore.

Type of energy... .no... not type – intensity! Could it be?!

He jumped up and ran to the back of the shuttle where he opened the hatch that lead to the shuttles reactor.

Please be intact. Please be intact!

He hadn't checked the reactor core before, because it was clearly in no condition to fly. It could still be functioning – at least he hoped that was the case.

It was not.

The scream of frustration that burst out of him seemed to tear apart the hanger on its own. Rage, desperation and frustration filled him. He was so close. Was the universe really that cruel? Failure at the very last moment?

He ran out of the shuttle, the relic in one hand, a scanner in the other. His determination made his teeth grit.

I've got this. I can do this. I just need another energy resource to test my theory. I will see this through to the end. I owe them this much. I owe it to myself.

The following ship he checked didn't work out either, its reactor was burned out. The next one had exploded, leaving a hole where its core should have been. One checked a third and a fourth, both without a positive result. He screamed out in anger and exhaustion as he ran towards the fifth shuttle. It seemed at this point he was just somehow moving a corpse he was trapped in. No matter how bad he felt, the shuttle he was heading for looked worse. Broken or destroyed would have been positive adjectives for the mess he was looking at. It seemed as if a gigantic fist had punched it repeatedly.

At this point it really doesn't matter anymore – so why not?

He entered the huge pile of metal junk that was once a shuttle. He had to duck down to reach the hold which would give him access to the ships reactor.

Here goes nothing...

He opened the hatch and couldn't help but stare down at what had to be one of the most intact looking reactors he had ever seen. It looked brand new and functional. With the pile of junk it inherited it wouldn't go anywhere of course, but it was exactly what he needed. He had to chuckle at the bizarre situation of kneeling inside a metal disaster, while connecting the relic to one of the last functioning energy sources in the hangar.

Now let's see if I was right – one last chance.

With sweaty hands he connected the relic to the reactor core. An insane plan, given what he had seen the relic do with energy, but this was his only chance.

He looked at his sensors and glanced at the energy signature of the relic. Silently he closed his eyes and got himself ready for an explosion, or at least a wave of energy that would tear the skin from his bones.

Nothing happened.

He opened his eyes and look at the readings. The relic's signature was exactly what he imagined it to be. Completely smooth.

So it is true.

He had finally figured out the last secret, the one missing link to put it all together.

The relic is a power amplifier, not a power transformer! I was wrong the whole time, thinking that it would take in energy to feed itself.

The relic does not feed on power, it amplifies the energy. It takes the form of whatever energy source is the nearest and strongest. That's why it built up such a destructive potential when it was near the spark nebula. Whenever it is not connected to a steady source of power it just takes in the wild energy sources of its surroundings, therefore getting completely out of control.

If it's connected to a harmonious source of power however... it's a completely different story.

The relic takes in the constant waves of energy and potentiates it into a multiple of its original unit. This problem is at the same time the solution. The destruction and chaos the relic is capable of, is directly correlated with the created energy and its output.

One smiled as his eyes filled with tears of joy. He had done it. He figured it out. He figured out how to get everything back in order, make everything right again. The sense of relief and sudden inner peace nearly became too much to handle before a sudden reality-check by the deafening sound of an alarm system. The ship shook and it seemed as if the Mothership itself was shaken by a huge invisible power, throwing it back and forth like a little boat out on the open sea.

One was thrown against the wall of the broken shuttle and the air was pushed out of his lungs leaving him breathless and in shock. He tried to get back on his feet when the ship rumbled and threw One off balance once again. The blustering sound of the alarm system blasted through every corner of the hanger, feeding the panic that was growing inside of One.

What is happening!?

On his hands and knees, One crawled out of the shuttle, relic clenched to his chest. As soon as he was out in the hanger again he looked around desperately to make sense of what was happening. His eyes caught the holoscreen of a nearby terminal that was suddenly displaying a waring in big red letters: WARNING – DANGER. SHIP ON COLLISION COURSE. EVACTUATE IMMIDIATLY.

Collision course?! Collision with what?

How could a drifting ship be on a course to anywhere? The ships engines weren't working.

The nebula!

One ran to the spot where he had entered the hangar after his desperate space dive and looked out into the open space. The ship was moving indeed, and it was moving faster than it should. It was not drifting anymore, it was going in a definite direction – into the nebula.

The ship must have gotten into the gravitation well of the nebula. This is bad... if it continues it will be crushed at the core of the nebula. The energy signature must have made the systems think it's another ship or something solid.

There was no time to lose, no matter what the system said what warnings it displayed, One new that there would be no collision but a complete overload of all systems, the reactor and even before the ship itself would be cave under the enormous gravity, the relic would definitely send out waves of energy that would be strong enough to crack the ship open like a nutshell.

He ran.

One left all his sensors and scanners behind, ignoring all the tools he had brought with him. There was no use for them anymore. This was it. This was the final stage of this nightmare. He had to get to the machine deck. There was only one thing left to do.

He ran.

The ship roared and moaned, as it was shaken again and again by the pull of the nebula. Corridors seemed like endless pipes, trays like the never ending journey through a constantly downsizing tunnel. He climbed, he ran, he crawled and he jumped.

A few hydraulic elevators and overhead railways that where still fuelled with some rest-energy of the ship helped him speed up his desperate journey to his final destination, but One could feel time slipping through his fingers. No matter how fast he moved, he felt like he was not fast enough.

As he was standing in another elevator that miraculously still worked, he tried to catch his breath and centre himself. The ship shook violently and he could hear glass bursting, cables break, metal bend and walls break down.

The elevator came to an abrupt stop before reaching its destination. The power had gone out and One needed to improvise. The elevator itself was one of many in a very large tunnel that connected multiple levels. There was a small platform opposite to the elevator that led to a few ladders which One could climb the rest of the way, but the platform was too far away. Especially while holding on to the relic with one arm.

I can make that jump. I have to make it.

Without any hesitation, he hit the glass of the elevator window as hard as he could. A little crack appeared but otherwise the glass seemed to withstand the attempt. In anger he hit against the window again and again. A sharp pain ran through his hand, but One no longer cared. He put all his strength into the next blow and shattered the window. His knuckles were bleeding, his hand was a bloody mess, and he couldn't care less.

One jumped.

When he hit the small platform he instinctively rolled away to lessen the impact to his knees.

The climb was hard, since he had to secure the relic with one arm. He tried to use his bleeding hand to climb but quickly realised the pain was too much and he had to switch to his healthy hand. He clenched the relic to his chest as tight as he could and started to climb. Halfway through, the ship shook once more, metal screeching all around him. He held on to the ladder, but his strength started to fade. When he thought the worst was over and he relaxed his grip ever so slightly, another blow ran through the ship, shaking the whole tunnel and hitting One unprepared. His wounded hand couldn't hold the relic firm enough and it slipped out of his hand.

The relic fell.

With absolute panic in his eyes, One watched the relic fall all the way down to the platform again and with a deafening unnatural sound that rang in One's ears like the sound of a deformed and grotesque church bell the relic hit the ground. It did not break. The platform did.

Stunned One looked at the platform that now had cracks running through it.

What is this thing made of!?

He climbed down again as quickly as he could to get the relic and start his climb up again. It seemed to take foverer, and as he climbed down and back up again the shakings increased in frequency.

He was close to the ships core, but time seemed to be running out.

Again he ran.

Corridors started to bend behind him, footways broke down, bridges collapsed. He ignored it all.

There is still time. I can still make it!

The ship was giving way to the crushing gravity and the walls around him seemed to slowly bend to its will. One ran as fast as his feet would carry him. The relic still pressed against his chest. His chest started to hurt because he pressed it so hard against himself that it nearly felt like a part of him. Maybe it was? His fate was connected to the relic and whatever would happen to it would decide his own life.

I am part of the relic and it is part of me. I will see us both through this.

The whole ship seemed to be falling apart when he finally reached his destination. He was standing at the edge of gigantic room that held the ships reactor. In any other situation, One would have been in awe of the impressive view, but now was not the time.

I have to get to the core. I gave to reach the reactor!

The pathway to the centre of the room was still intact, but as One entered it to reach the room another shock ran through the ship and every step he took was not only closer to the reactor but also farther away from the collapsing pathway behind him. His steps got more desperate, but they also got slower. He was at the end of what his body could take. Behind him the last passageway collapsed and fell down to the far away bottom of the room. There was no way back now. He looked forward and saw the reactor. It was not far away but all pathways down leading to the reactor where gone. Frail as they had been they all seemed to have collapsed with the last big shaking of the ship. The only way to the reactor would be from the bottom of the room upwards, but he not only did not have the time to get to the lower levels and reach the reactor from underneath, he literally couldn't go back anymore since the bridge had collapsed.

The reactor was so close, yet unreachable, levitating in its frame above bottom of the room. Unreachable without the pathway bridges leading to it. He looked at the reactor. It hummed with power. Slowly, steadily, peacefully. It waited for whatever fate was awaiting. Close enough to see it clearly, too far down to reach it, all though the distance was not that big.

I could try to throw the relic, but I am not sure it would really reach the reactor. The brief contact may not be enough for the relic to react to the new energy source. There has to be another way...

One only could think of one realistic way to bring it to an end. He felt a strange urge, just as if the relic itself told him what to do. As if it had known his plan all along. He looked down at it, still pressed against his chest – the source of all troubles, but at this very moment it felt more like a new-born to him.

In that instant, he noticed that the relic was glowing. One was unsure what was happening, there was no energy source around. It certainly was not the reactor, because it was too far away.

You know what to do. It is time.

As the realization set in, he felt a strange feeling of relief and redemption.

For the mission. For the ship.

He jumped.

The reactor came closer with every heartbeat. It rushed towards him. All his interactions with the relic flashed before his eyes, and with one last breast he turned his back to the reactor he was falling towards and faced the relic one last time.

For the Crew. For my friends. Peace at least.

His body hit the outer wall of the reactor and the world seemed to explode into an inferno of glistening luminance.

Then darkness swallowed everything.

NINE

RAREFORM

Silhouettes moved at the corner of his eyes. He tried to open them further, but nothing happened. All he could see was a very distant light – it seemed so far away. He could hear voices speaking. Two voices. Where was he? Was he alive? What had happened?

"He is getting better... not the running-around-feeling-awesome kind of better, but at least he now has a chance."

"This is way too risky, I am telling you this is too dangerous. We still don't know what we are dealing with and who says this thing is going to stay as stable as it is now?"

"Look at the readings. That thing is running smooth and quiet, our systems are boosted and the ship is doing great, despite what it has been through."

"I still think it's too dangerous. We should look for ways to destroy that thing as soon as possible or leave it somewhere in the deepest, darkest corner of the universe."

"It's the most fascinating amplifier we have ever seen. This thing boosts this ship in levels we couldn't even imagine! Just look at how well the repairs are going!"

"It amplifies human energy as well, man! I say it is too dangerous!"

Amplifies human energy?

He wanted to say something, wanted to shout, to ask, but his body would not have any of it. Darkness swallowed him again and the silhouettes faded.

Am I alive?

Again the distant light. It looked like a bar of light on the horizon. He tried to focus, tried to get control over his body, but he couldn't. He couldn't even feel it anymore. It felt like he was a passenger in whatever form of existence this was.

Again he could see silhouettes. This time they seemed to be little clearer. There were more of them now. He could hear voices again, but he couldn't figure out if they were the same he had heard before.

Where am I?!

"Have you seen it?"

"Yes."

"So?"

"I don't know."

"Oh, don't give me that shit again."

"Look, I don't know, ok!? What do you want me to say? I have no idea why his condition got worse. I mean it seems like...

but that's crazy talk... still... it seems like he is healing with the ship."

"What do you mean, he is healing with the ship?"

"Exactly that. I don't know how... but somehow he seems almost connected to the ship in some way. I cannot say what the best way to proceed would be. I have seen a lot of crazy shit, but this? No clue. I just hope the others will have more luck in their research. I hate to step around in the dark."

"Yeah, same here."

"We should see if we can get..."

His mind was fading again. His focus was exhausted. Darkness welcomed him with open arms.

Silhouettes again. He didn't even try to open his eyes anymore. He felt tired. So tired. Why don't they let him sleep? Or maybe they did? Who are they anyway? Who was he? Where was he? When was or what was he?

No answers and no one to ask.

All he could do was to listen to the voices again and maybe catch a clue about his situation. This time there were more voices.

"....so how does he do it?"

"Do what?"

"Whatever is happening to his body, he has to have some sort of power over it right?"

"I really don't think so."

"I mean, he is out most of the time. What do you expect him to control?"

"Never mind the fact that he is a floating corpse in a gravity field."

"You could be a little more respectful. After all, he did save us. He was ready to sacrifice himself for us."

"...and he was the person that brought us into this mess in the first place. Now I'm expected to show gratitude for him solving a problem he himself created?"

"We all knew the risks of going on such a mission. We never blamed him for it. We shouldn't start with it now."

"I know... you are right. Sorry. Just... I mean... look at him!"

"We can see it, but at this point there is nothing we can do. Whatever happens to him will have to happen without us understanding it."

"I think it's saving him."

"That's impossible."

"Everything we saw was impossible."

"Yes. That is true. Scientifically we are at an end."

"Just because we can't explain it does not make it a miracle. This technology is far more complex than any of us would have imagined."

He tried to move, but nothing happened. He could definitely feel that something in his body was happening, but he did not feel any movement. It was as if his body was covered in something incredibly heavy that kept him from moving.

"...you know we don't have the means to explain it to him right now, and at this point we don't even know if he will ever get out of this... whatever state it is that he is in."

"Unconsciousness?"

"No. That's the mystery here. He is not completely knocked out. He is just... not completely here either."

"Like he's in a fever or something."

"That is actually very close to the truth. Seems like he's in a delirium."

"The question is: Is he getting better or worse?"

"I think it is getting better, but can't say for sure. Just by the sight in front of me I instantly question my own theories."

"Well, only time will tell I guess."

Only time will tell, but how much time does it need? And how much time has passed?

His body felt heavy. His mind felt heavy. He felt his mind drifting away again.

Please let me wake up. I want to wake up. I want to wake up!

This time he knew that he was dreaming, although he was completely aware of himself. It was a dream. He was in the reactor room again. Holding the relic. Falling – falling forever – the relic clutched against his body. He looked down just to see it melting into his body, into his chest and slowly covering his upper body, then his legs and feet until the only thing free was his face. With nothing to hold anymore he spread his arms and legs. He was falling into the heart of the nebula. There was the Mothership, awaiting his landing. At the very centre it floated and he knew it was his destination. It always had been.

It's time.

He opened his eyes to finally wake up from the beyond he had roamed.

At first, the light seemed unbearable. Like a supernova that burned itself into his skull, but with every passing second he could make out more and more of the room he was in, and the people surrounding him.

The Crew.

Commander Swayton, Sid, Ermis, Michael, Fèanis and the Captain, Jörg. They were all there, looking at him with mixed feelings. None of their faces was hardened with anger or judgement.

"Welcome back."

Swaytons smiled at him, although One could see the concern in his eyes.

"I won't lie... there were times when I thought you'd never wake up."

They all seemed to ease up a little, now that the first ice had been broken, but Sid and Ermis still seemed a little tense, so did Fèanis, who looked at him as if he couldn't believe what he saw, but also with a hint of fascination.

"You have been gone for a while," Fèanis spoke softly, "it is good to have you back with us."

"To be honest we kind of thought you're a goner for sure," Ermis said with a warm smile.

"Well, I mean, we all thought we were goners for sure," Sid added with a wide grin.

One could only think of one thing to say.

"Is the ship safe?'

"Yes, it is safe. You did saved it. You saved us."

Jörg stepped towards him, his face covered in a tired kindness.

"As the others said, we had great concerns for your health, to put it mildly. Some time has passed since you made that jump into the reactor."

"How do you know that? I mean, the jump?" One asked in surprise.

"Funny enough with the whole ship falling apart, a few cameras were still up and running. One of them was in the reactor room. We watched the whole thing, and when we saw you jump... to be frank... we all held our breaths because we didn't know what you were trying to achieve with that suicide jump."

For a moment Jörg seemed almost angry, although One noticed that the anger was not directed at him.

"In the end you saved us all – and for that we are grateful. More than you can imagine. You willingly risked everything to save the ship and our cause. Whatever our concerns were, you did the right thing and you made the right calls at the end."

The others nodded in agreement.

But what did I actually do?

"What... what happened after I jumped. What did I do? Did the relic respond to the reactor? Was my theory correct?"

They all fell silent. Many looked at the floor as if in shame or guilt and tried to avoid looking at him.

"One – please take a look around you," Fèanis said. He had not taken his eyes off him, and his stare was intense. One did as he was told and realized where he was and why the Crew seemed uncomfortable. It was not guilt, it was pity. They felt sorry for him and now he could see why.

One was floating in a force field, but not in the hospital ward or in an emergency room. The room he was in didn't look like he was even near the medical section of the ship. There was nothing in the room but the force field, and a lot of equipment One was not familiar with. None of it really looked like medical gear.

"Where am I?!" he demanded.

"You are in an extra room we quickly prepared for you while we waited for you to wake up. We are near the reactor room more precisely." Jörg's face stayed friendly as he spoke, although One could feel the tension in his body increase.

"But why am I here? Are the medical facilities of the ship damaged?"

"No, but nothing there would have been able to help you. We couldn't help you. Commander, if you would be so kind." Jörg said as he motion to Commander Swayton.

"You see, first we did everything we could to get you into an emergency room and tend to your wounds. We did everything we could. Trust me, everything. The state of your body was so unique that our conventional methods were all in vain. In an act of sheer desperation we came up with the idea of bringing you back here. Close to the core."

The unique state of my body? What?

"The state of my body? What happened to me?!"

Swayton gestured him to look down and so he did. What he saw was more than he could take. His scream echoed through the room and met the Crew's silence.

"We are sorry, One. We are so sorry."

His body was covered with something strange and mechanical. It was a white surface, flawless and shimmering. Although it didn't cover all of his body, it gave him a strange biochemical look. Sensors were attached to his body parts, mainly the ones covered with the substance. The closer he looked at it, the more familiar it became until he realized that this wasn't some strange substance or even mechanical parts. It was so much more.

"The relic," One whispered.

"Yes," Swayton answered, "the relic has not only connected itself to the core... it has somehow reacted to you as well. It seems like you were the catalyst that made it possible for the relic to harness the core's power. Although we don't know how this happened, somehow your body was the bridge needed to combine the relic with the ship's core."

"So the ships energy..."

"...is stronger than ever before. The repairs are nearly done, and we do not have to look for another power source. You didn't just save the ship, you improved it."

"...for a price," Jörg said with a sense of sadness in his voice.

"A price you were willing to pay without hesitating," Ermis added, his voice raised.

"The thing is, we couldn't heal you through standard medical procedures," Swayton continued, "but as soon as we brought you close to the core you immediately started to get better. So we kept you here and we actually saw you regenerating without us even needing to take further actions."

One tried to take it all. Panic fought its way to the surface.

"What does that all mean?!" he exclaimed.

For a few seconds everyone was quiet, until Fèanis stated what One already knew deep inside but was just too scared to say out loud.

"It means that you heal through and with the ship. You are linked to it. The relic is linked to it. And you are linked to each other."

One knew that the words were true. He knew it was what had happened.

"We cannot explain everything. Our knowledge on the relic remains very limited, but we know that there is a way to remove that link between you and the ship, somehow. You gave us this energy source, and we used it to power up the ship again. We're safe thanks to you. Now that you're regenerated, we believe it is safe to remove the relic from your body and turn you into your old self again. We already ran a number of tests and we are confident that we can get you back to normal."

"So I will have my body back? Fully functional?" One asked.

"Yes, but it will take time."

"You'll be running around gathering other relics to destroy the Mothership in no time," Sid said with a big smile on his face.

"There is another possibility though." Fèanis said with a

suddenly grim tone.

As Fèanis stepped forward, One could see the rest of the Crew getting tense. Ermis turned to Fèanis whispered sharply, "you know it is too soon. We can't ask this of him. It is too much."

"The codex spoke of things like this and we have to consider it. You know this as well as I do," Fèanis answered.

"You know I am always on your side when it comes to these things," Ermis replies, "but for fuck's sake Fèanis, you cannot ask someone to give up his humanity for the fucking codex. This is our responsibility not his."

Jörg interrupted them harshly, "Ermis, please let him speak. We talked about this and I know you think it is too much, I even tend to agree with you, but Fèanis has a point as well and you know this. It's up to One, and he should have the chance to at least consider it."

Fèanis gave Ermis one last glance, a small nod to make it clear that no grudge was between them. One knew that there was something dividing the Crew at this moment but even so they did not fail to respect each other.

"One," Fèanis said, "you have another possibility. You can become one with the ship."

Complete silence. No one seemed to even breathe.

"How... how would that be possible?"

"We do not remove the parts of the relic from your body and let you and the ship stay connected. It's a symbiosis that makes you become one with the ship – lets you feel and power it through this link. It gives you more insight on the Mothership than any of us could ever have and it makes you unique to our cause. You would help us more than we can explain. You would become part of something bigger."

"You have this choice, because you believed in our cause, our mission, and we know that you seek something beyond the world you already know," Jörg added, "this is your choice and no one will make it for you. Not one person in this room holds any resentment towards you for what has happened and we will never ask you to do something you do not want to do yourself. With everything that has come to pass we do not want any kind of reparations from you. You do not have to make up for anything. I hope you know that."

"How can you say that!?," One burst into tears as the whole reality of what had happened washed over him. "I nearly killed us all! I nearly destroyed this ship with my obsession and my hunger for knowledge. I put us all in danger because I was selfish! How can you not be angry or disappointed? I don't understand this – why are you so forgiving, when I was the one to put us all in danger?!"

This time the silence stretched out for what seemed to be an eternity before Jörg spoke again.

"We all knew the risks. We all knew the dangers. We trusted you as much as we trusted everyone else on this journey. You made a mistake. You lost your way. But you know what? So did all of us at one point and that is what this journey is about. If we were perfect from top to bottom we never would have left Gaia in the first place. We learn and we grow beyond our past selves. With all that happened, what matters most is that you never hesitated to make things right again, and were ready to risk everything to do so. You put the mission and the ship before yourself for this entire time and we know this."

As tears ran down his cheeks One could do nothing but thank the Crew.

"Think about what you want and what is important to you. This journey will not stop here and we won't leave you behind. You will continue as an important part of this cause in whatever way you want. This has always been what the Mothership was about," Jörg concluded.

After Jörg's words, the Crew left One with his thoughts.

A long time One silently floated in his force field. The only sound keeping him company was the humming of the sensors and machines.

As he looked up after being lost in thoughts forever, he noticed one of the holoscreens at the wall. It showed the footage of the Mothership's exocams. The ship was softly gliding into a nebula to gather its energy. Somehow, One already knew that. He could feel it. Every part of his body felt the warm sensation and excitement as the energy from the gasses in the nebula was harnessed by the ship. It was as if he gently walked into an ocean of warm water. For the first time in his life One felt at peace. The hunger inside him, the constant search for knowledge had stopped, as he saw millions of stars in front of his eyes as if he was drifting in space himself. Whole galaxies opened up in front of him and the universe seemed to greet him with open arms. He was home. He was finally where he belonged.

One realized that he could never get back to his old self. He didn't want to leave this link with the universe. This ship had saved him just as he had saved it, and with all they had been through they now were one.

The Crew had never needed to forgive him, because they never blamed him in the first place. With everything he had done to make this right, it was time he forgave himself. It was time to look into the present, the future – not the past. The future was ready to be experienced and it was no longer his escape from reality, but his link to happiness. He had faced the wrongs he had done and he had made it right in the end. It was time to become something more, something greater – something eternal. It was time to outgrow the individual that followed a cause and become the cause itself. The ship was his home, his body and he was its soul.

He was one with himself. One with the cause. One with the ship. One with the love and acceptance that he had been given and shown. One with the Crew. One with his mistakes and flaws. He was the Mothership and he was the universe with all its living beings.

We are the Mothership.

And we are One.

TEN

LET THIS STORM CARRY US HOME

To Whom It May Concern,
a data log on the topic of Dark Matter and Ascension.

What makes a member of the Mothership? What makes us continue in our journey though the stars, when our hope has faded? What is our cause if not the combined effort of everyone involved?

I witnessed an individual that I deemed broken and done, rise to a level that I thought impossible and I rebuke myself for not believing in the capability of this ship and its Crew as I used to. When One carried the relic to the core and took the jump I couldn't help but think about our true self and where our real strength comes from. While we honour science and the search for knowledge we so often are blind to the heart of our journey. To believe in something that goes beyond our single minds and bodies, something greater that connects us and fuels our will and our determination to actually make a difference.

In his act of selflessness we actually saw what the human body and mind are capable of. The reason we left Gaia is embodied in One's leap of faith. Not faith in an invisible higher power he bows down to or bends his knee for. Not the obedience towards the Crew. The faith One showed on that day was about believing in life and matter. The link between us all in this journey is vital for its success. We will never come as far as we hope to if there is a lack of trust and faith in our humanity, in our community and our bond.

We are just a tiny blip in the eternity of the galaxy. Everything that happened – or almost happened – to us, pales in comparison to the sorrows of the universe. Even though the universe itself probably took little notice of the things that transpired on the Mothership it surely felt the victory that day. The victory of a single person that overcame all fears and doubts to become something more than before. Without a seemingly small victory like that, no journey would be worth the taking. A bigger picture is always made out of small details and no one ever heard of a good cause that didn't live from the individual journeys of its followers.

I tend to remind myself of this every day while facing what lies ahead. A lot has happened and I know that the trials ahead will demand everything from us. To walk in One's path is to understand that our lives are not defined by our mistakes, but by our presence. Nothing is lost as long as we understand the impact of our soul on this plane of existence. We can change our fate as much as we can change what lies ahead of us, and the strength I seek in these dark days lies not in fearing the horrifying path ahead but being present in every step towards reaching the end of this dark journey.

I know my friends and members of the Crew are fighting their own battles right now and we all do our part do get through this nightmare day by day. Hope is not yet lost and whatever I will encounter I will face with trust in my soul, trust in us – trust in the Mothership. On dark days I close my eyes in fond memories of One, who sacrificed so much to do what he thought was right and just. I can only hope for the same strength he displayed to win the fight that lies ahead of us.

We may be separated for now, but I know I will see my the Crew again. I will not let One's actions go in vain. Eternity is ours. The Mothership will prevail and so will the people joined in our cause. For we will not cower in fear of this Dark Matter that tears at our hopes, but make our own leap of faith to form the link that symbolizes our Ascension.

I shall call this chapter of our journey Of Dark Matter And Ascension hoping to create the pillar of light that gives hope to us in the coming times, when we have to fight our own war to create the future we set out to find."

Fèanis,

Last Keeper of the Codex. Days of the Regicide.

A few years ago I started to put together a concept about a topic every human can relate to: crisis. When the world comes down on you, how do you react? What are your mind and psyche doing?

My partner and her mother, both professionals in the field of psychiatry, supported me greatly in coming up with scientifically correct framework of the states the human mind experiences when in crisis. This was important, because, as a creative collective, we believe in the scientific method and base our work on that.

One goes through his downfall, builds himself up again and rises with a clear vision of what his personal purpose should. He commits to a cause bigger than himself. Kind of like the members of CALL THE MOTHERSHIP do on and off stage, to grow and continue this project.

For example, Thomas Fèanis played a very important role in the creation of this novel. He committed a lot of personal time and energy to grasp the meaning and the essence of the concept and to put it in words, that I was not able to find. When I say, he did a great job with that, then this is an understatement. I cannot wrap my head around the fact that he was able to put my formless idea into words about the human essence itself covering nearly 100 pages. That's the same with all the other members in this project. In fact, they all understand the direction and know me so well, that they can always manifest my thoughts.

Even though we're all are just motivated amateurs, it would be a lot harder to provide this level of quality without the professional guidance of Peter Gordebeke, the only real scientist in this creative collective. He always makes sure that our written word and our visual identity are consistent, and in the case of this novel, that the language is better than just par for the course.

For the last 3 years, "OF DARK MATTER AND ASCENSION" was the main topic for CALL THE MOTHERSHIP. Every bit of output and content was a part of this huge mosaic, and with this novel we close the door on the biggest chapter of this project so far. I want to thank everyone involved, especially my band for supporting and creating art and everyone in our orbit for participating this very journey of ours.

See you on the other side.

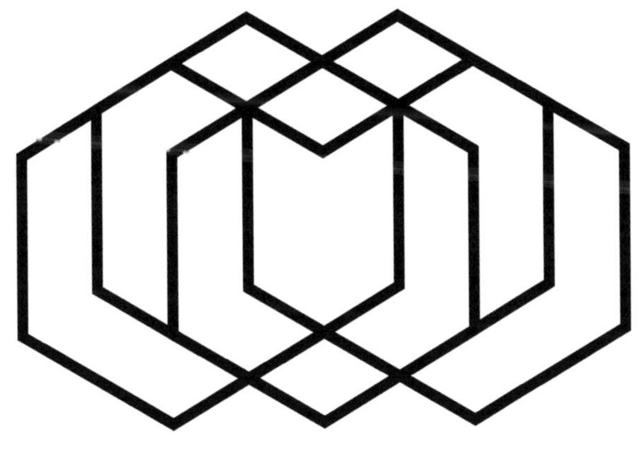

CALL THE **MOTHERSHIP**